Sweet

Sweet Justice

P.O.N.D. Casebook No.1

To Kaylah

Daily see yourself.
See yourself the way the world sees you.

Enjoy,
Gabriella

For information on future titles and to delve deeper into

Sweet Crime, Sweet Justice:

www.gabriellagordon.co.uk

Facebook: GabriellaGordonAuthor

Instagram: @gabriellagordonauthor

Sweet Crime, Sweet Justice

P.O.N.D. Casebook No.1

GABRIELLA GORDON

ISBN: 978-1-3999-1286-0

For H and C,
the lights of my life,
my purpose for everything.

hello world

Introduction

Ingleby Arncliffe is a real place.

I know because I grew up there. I'm not E.G, but do I know how she must feel living there. It's a magical place - in so many senses of the word. You make dens hidden down Green Lane, you sneak into a water tower when it's not allowed and know you'll never forget its inky blackness. You find friends who come in and out of your life, and then stay for good. You go on secret adventures in the middle of the night, where you revel in the freedom and just eat toffees. (Sometimes your friend will get caught by their mum, sometimes they won't.) Then all these experiences become part of you, and one day your imagination quietly wisps and wends and you create characters and adventures that you wish were real. And the magic starts again...

Chapter 1

The Unnecessary Saving

"Every time! Every time!" he muttered to himself, finding it beyond belief that *yet again* he'd managed to get himself into a bit of a pickle. In fact, he was probably in a whole jar of pickles. Though pickled what, he didn't know. His round black eyes came together in a frown. Did it have to be a vegetable? He didn't know that either. But he was sure about the pickle bit.

Desperate not to be found like this, and feeling indignant that small branches had the nerve to prod him in places that he could never bring himself say out loud, he gave his sturdy backside a shake. At first just with a suggestion of a flourish, then, when this didn't work, he did it again but with a real, proper, actual flourish. Nothing. Why did he *always* get stuck here?! With a grimace, he pulled out what had to be his best bottom shimmy. How could that not work? But it didn't. Not one teeny, tiny, nano millimetre further forwards. He let out a heavy sigh.

Gritting his teeth, he now engaged his backside with what could be termed full and affirmative gusto. No. Still in the hole! Was he ever going to make it through? His shoulders slumped to the ground and he muttered comments about the ridiculousness of his situation - which surprisingly had no effect either. Having used up all his normal tactics, he decided he may as well just breathe in.

So, in an attempt to make his lower half as deflated and therefore flat as possible, he tried to suck up all the air to the top of his body. At the same time, he pushed his short arms above his head, urging them forwards as far as they would go, his screwed-up face scuffling around in the dirt. He reached till his fingers, and his ears, hurt from the strain. The ear pain was usually a good sign.

Suddenly: Ugh! Oomph! Pop! He was through. Sprawled out on his re-inflated, rather generous stomach in the damp mud, but most importantly he was through. He had triumphed over the little arch at the foot of the leafy hedge. He scowled back over his shoulder at the innocent twigs. He then briskly stood up and, with a bit of head rocking, tried to look as if nothing had just happened. Glancing casually round, he checked that no-one had noticed his less-than-slick entrance. There was never anyone about, but he always checked because he *always* got stuck in the entrance hole in the stupid hedge. He wasn't quite sure why it even happened. Absent-mindedly he patted his round stomach as he pondered the question.

Having left the bright sunshine behind, he now stood in a dark tunnel of trees. As he glanced up, he thought again how the broad, mossy branches arching together looked like the vaulted ceiling of an old church. Beneath his small feet, the dense undergrowth gave off the rich, earthy scent that he loved. His long furry, nose twitched indulgently.

Drawing in a big breath to brace himself, he pivoted carefully round to face the annoying hedge that he'd just popped through. Rolling back his shoulders like a gymnast preparing for action, he took two measured side-steps to the right. He quickly reached out to clasp the thick horizontal root. It ran like a handrail along the base of the hedgerow. Stiff-backed, he peered to his right where the ground sloped steeply down to a murky brook. He took a nervous step onto the slope. Instantly his short hind legs scrambled frantically to get a foothold, like he was cycling an invisible bike. But the soil simply crumbled beneath him. More mutterings, this time about the poor earth quality in this area. With his green tweed waistcoat planted in the mud and legs dangling forlornly, he clung grimly to the hand-rail root. He let himself hang for a minute as he tried to catch his breath. It was usually at this point that he asked himself why he came this way. And the answer was never any different: laziness. Not that he would ever admit that to anyone.

If his friend found this way in 'a walk in the park' - well, easy - so could he. And besides, it all

9

seemed too much of an effort to come the long way round: to trudge the full length of three fields, all of which somehow seemed to have just been ploughed. Only then to have to battle his way through rigid, and it must be said, rather predatory brambles, which inevitably caught on his spines. And in the unlikely event that he managed that, then actually remember the best way through a tangled copse of trees. All without being seen by the locals. No, he told himself, he was more than capable of this more 'athletic' route!

Gripping both his paws tighter around the gnarled root he dug his feet into the muddy bank. The root creaked and bent threateningly. He stepped gingerly, and hopefully (he was always hopeful in pickled situations) sideways along the 'cliff face' – well, the one metre bank of the quite small brook. Instantly, he was on his well-proportioned stomach, again, his short, thickset arms stretched above him, just about holding on. The bulge in his waistcoat pocket attracted further clumps of mud, as it always did. He never had to actually look over his shoulder to see the cold water only a few feet below him to know that the tumble wasn't so much painful as humiliating. He and this muddy brook were not friends.

At last, he'd shuffled to the narrowest section of the brook. But he couldn't relax yet. He had to leap to the other side of the water. He now needed to be nimble. Though 'nimble' never actually happened -

ever. Grimacing, he turned his body to face the brook, an arm outstretched behind him. Then, still gripping the root tightly with his left hand, he got ready to launch himself. But at the last moment he felt his foot slip. Just as he braced himself for the inevitable, undignified splat into the cold, brown water, he felt a sharp tug on the back of his waistcoat. For a minute he thought he'd caught it on the root, but then a smooth, velvet voice floated up from behind him,

"Steady, little spiky one. You do not wish to end up in there I assume."
He was then deftly lifted over to the other side of the brook. He landed gently and, bewildered, turned to see a rather large pink rabbit standing in front of him. His brain scrambled to find words. The only thing he could think of to say was 'pink', but he knew he couldn't just say that. But before he could get his brain in gear the *pink* rabbit said,

"Righty-o. You are most welcome." And as he hopped off, he called back over his shoulder, "But do not tell all the hedgehogs, or they shall all want saving!"

Hedgehog half-raised his arm as if to say something, albeit a little too late, but he still couldn't get past the word *pink*. He shook his head trying to loosen up his thoughts and walked slowly round the three large beech trees - which he and his friend EG had cleverly named Three Trees. It was these and the copse of smaller trees behind them that kept their headquarters hidden from the village. Hedgehog knew all he had to do was get to the small pond and EG would help him work out what had just happened. He could rely on her to get his brain back in order. Summer sunlight dappled gently down through Three Trees. Even though their top-secret headquarters was so top-secret, it never seemed dark there. In fact, it always seemed to Hedgehog as if the light actually found them. As he approached Sutton's Pond, he was surprised to hear that same smooth, velvet voice:

"I have come in response to your advertisement."

He heard EG's voice, puzzled, "What advertisement?"

"On your website."

"Website?" EG asked, a little vaguely.

"Yes. It is a place of information on a computer that-"

"I know what a website is!" Now irritated, as she prided herself on being a proper techie.

The rabbit smiled. EG found her irritation instantly vanished.

"I apologise EG, of course you do."

Hedgehog walked purposefully up and interrupted.

"Hi EG," he threw a sideways glance at the *pink* rabbit then ignored him. "It's stopped!"

"What! Completely?" She now turned to Hedgehog, though kept flicking her dark eyes back at the smiling rabbit, who stood quite complacently beside her.

"Yes, there hasn't been any vandalism on the house for the last three days. Fenella is *so* relieved. She's found it really stressful." Hedgehog didn't admit that it wasn't just his wife who had been very stressed by having their house vandalised by an unknown person, but he had too. "So there's no need for us to investigate, no more mystery. Hope they're all like this!"

"That's great. But, you know, I would've liked to have found out who did it." EG chewed her lip as she spoke.

"I did this."

Stunned, they both stared at the rabbit.

"What!" cried EG. It took a second for Hedgehog to exclaim because he was again thrown by the pinkness of the rabbit.

"What! You vandalised my house-"

"Well-" began the pink rabbit.

"You almost destroyed the home that my wife and I-"

"I-"

"-have lived in since we married? The home where our children-"

This time the rabbit forced his voice over Hedgehog's. "I did not mean that I was the culprit, the vandal himself. Rather, I think that it was I that brought such actions to cease, to end."

Hedgehog stopped abruptly. "Oh." Then narrowed his eyes. "What do you mean?"

"Well, it was indeed three days ago that I was passing a large oak tree with a small, green door (Hedgehog nodded; his house had a green door) and found a young man to be throwing stones at the tree and kicking it quite fearsomely. I spoke to him and explained how unacceptable his actions were. He agreed and left. As I was walking away, I think I saw what must have been your good wife leave from the same green door. However, she moved a little too quickly for me to see where she went and thus explain. So, yes, I think I have put an end to your mystery." He smiled at the other two, looking quite pleased with himself.

Hedgehog frowned, "So, just like that, this person stopped?"

"Yes."

"You just told him to stop and he did?"

"Yes."

"Hmm. Doesn't sound right to me. What do you think EG?"

EG didn't seem to hear Hedgehog's question. She'd just been staring at the pink rabbit. He was about the same height as her, and she was quite tall for a ten-year-old. However, his long upright ears seemed to tower over her in a majestic way. She couldn't work out his fur: on the one hand it looked smooth and silky, yet it also looked fluffy and well worn. She wasn't quite sure how it could do that. But he did have a softness about him. Though she felt that this was not a rabbit that you readily cuddled - he seemed to command respect. He was definitely pink though - he was a pale bubble gum pink all over, except for his tummy which was a little lighter. That was more candy floss pink. And there was something familiar about him, but she couldn't quite place it. It would come to her, she knew.

"Who are you?" She felt herself compelled to ask. The pink rabbit had started meandering round the pond quietly taking in everything that he saw. At the question he turned and bounded over to her, holding out his hand, which EG shook.

"I am Pink Rabbit. I shall leave it to you to work out as to why I have such a wonderful name. But you can call me Pink Rabbit for short." His whiskers seemed to twitch wryly as he spoke.

Hedgehog snorted. "I suppose that's Rabbit with two ts – Rabbitt."

"Only if spelling is a challenge for you. One is sufficient – I have more than enough of other things."

Pink Rabbit hopped over to him, with hand again outstretched. As he shook Hedgehog's hand vigorously, he said, "And you must have a *very* interesting name."

"Well, er kind of, it's Hedgehog." Then quickly added, "Ah no, it's *Mr* Hedgehog actually." He held himself up a little taller, still only reaching the rabbit's shoulder.

"Ah yes, indeed very imaginative. Of course I shall call you Hedgehog."

Hedgehog opened his mouth to insist on 'Mr', then realised it would be pointless and he wasn't exactly sure if the rabbit was mocking him.

EG had been watching Hedgehog carefully as he had shaken hands with Pink Rabbit, because when the rabbit had shaken hers, she had felt a surge of energy running up her arm. At first, she'd thought it was an electric shock, but it was more like a warmth, a deep, intense warmth. It had confused her. Everything about this Pink Rabbit confused her. She saw Hedgehog promptly pull his hand away, but then Hedgehog just seemed annoyed by the rabbit. Pink Rabbit confused her, but also somehow, she felt better already for him being here – but again, she couldn't quite put her finger on why.

"Why are you pink? And why are you here?" EG was surprised by the unfriendly tone Hedgehog had when he spoke because he was normally such a friendly person.

"Why are any of us any colour? I am pink to highlight how special I am," he replied airily, smiling. Hedgehog scowled but said nothing. "As to why I am here, as I said earlier, I have come in response to your website advertisement. It said 'Investigative Services Offered: No Mystery Too Small. For Local Detectives please contact…' Nonetheless, I thought I should come in person to offer my investigative services for your detective agency. I am sure that you could use a third person on your team."

"No!" said Hedgehog.

"Yes," said EG at the same time.

Hedgehog stared at EG. "We don't need anyone else!"

"Well, he did solve The Mystery of the Vandal and that was our first mystery. It'd be fun to have someone else and we're bound to get loads of business," she said brightly. Hedgehog stared at EG again; she was not someone who liked the company of lots of people and was often wary of anyone new. He opened his mouth to say something but EG said, "Come on, I'll show you round." Her face alight with enthusiasm, she led Pink Rabbit to the back of the pond, to her shed. She stopped momentarily on the wooden decking in front of the shed as Pink Rabbit asked,

"So, is that your name, EG? An interesting name too."

"Well, it's not actually my full name, those are the initials of my first and middle name. And I hate both of them!"

"And what are your full names?"

"No, I don't tell anyone. Ever."

"I see. Yet, I often think if one denies one's name, one denies a part of oneself." He mused casually. "Well, maybe you are an 'example' to the world," he smiled. EG blushed, then frowned in an attempt to hide the blush.

"Er, I don't think so…" She opened the door to her wooden shed and they stepped inside. From the outside it was quite unassuming – a tumbledown looking thing. A bit forlorn, with scraps of wood nailed on to form patches over holes.

Inside was completely different. It was almost like another world. There were gadgets and tools everywhere. Running down the right side of the back wall was an array of shelves made from off-cuts of wood and almost straight branches. Each shelf was jam-packed with glass jars, battered boxes and old bottles that looked like they might well have been dug up from the ground. All the containers were carefully labelled: cap screws, wood screws, nails (10mm), glue gun, straws (plastic) and many other things that Pink Rabbit would have to look up in some technical book. Beneath the shelves hung tools on nail hooks, poised for action.

With shining eyes, EG watched Pink Rabbit as he stepped curiously towards the back wall. Fixed to the wall to the left of the shelves, was a large piece of MDF wood which had been painted with blackboard paint. On it was chalked: *Ideas*. And there were definitely 'ideas'! It was covered in sketches of gadgets in EG's scrawly writing and squeezed in any gap were swirls of mathematical calculations. Hurriedly pinned at the bottom of the board were overlapping scraps of notes – some referred to The

Mystery of the Vandal. Curious lumps of Blu-Tack were stuck in what must be strategic places around the room; easily available when EG might need them urgently. Everywhere Pink Rabbit looked there were items that EG had obviously decided were 'useful'. Something brushed the tip of his ear. He tipped his head back to see the rafters laden with rolls of tubing, coils of old rope and oily bicycle chains, dangling down, patiently waiting to be used.

Everything was there to do a job. A naked light bulb hung from a flex in the middle of the ceiling. To one side, EG had fashioned a small sink out of a metal bucket which sat neatly in a hole in a kitchen work top. A piece of hose arched up from behind the bucket and served as a tap. All you had to do was squeeze a small pump with your foot and water came gushing out. Next to the sink was a mini fridge. Just as Pink Rabbit was about to open a rather intriguing looking drawer, which bulged with items and didn't quite close properly, EG couldn't contain herself any longer and said with obvious pride,

"What d'you think?"

However, before he could answer she pointed to the front wall. "And you've got to look at this – it took me ages to put all this together." She pulled out a rickety old computer chair that seemed to be held together with Gaffa tape, and wheeled herself forward to another section of the work top. She'd made this space into a desk area so she could enjoy the view from the single window. She liked to look up at the pond and Three Trees and just think.

"This is an old Apple Mac but I just added a memory chip – people think you can't do that, but you just need to be really good at soldering, and I mean really good. This laptop I found in a skip, can you believe it? There was nothing wrong with it really, except the screen needed replacing, but that's easy to do yourself, if you know how." She spoke so fast that Pink Rabbit could hardly keep up with what she was saying, let alone understand the technicality of it all. He looked to the doorway to see Hedgehog leaning against the door frame, smiling a little smugly.

"It can be confusing," Hedgehog said, "if you're not very good at technology."

Pink Rabbit reached forward to a large metal box on the wall.

"Nonsense, I am very well versed in many areas of technology, this computer, for instance is-"

"Don't touch that!" yelled EG, standing so quickly that her wheeled chair crashed into the back of the shed. Pink Rabbit instantly snatched his hand away. "That's the terminal box to my generator. Anything happens to that and all my systems go down." She swung her arm across the room, to indicate the array screens, keyboards, switches and boxes, all with multi-coloured cables protruding from them. "I've got a small generator out the back of the shed – it's my lifeline really. It's how I power everything here and recharge all the basics." As she said 'basics' she nodded to the wall above the computer where there was an assortment of cameras, phones and other gizmos that perhaps only EG could identify.

"I do apologise. I can see clearly now the purpose of this box," said Pink Rabbit.

Hedgehog turned away, smirking to himself.

"That's OK," she said, patting the terminal box protectively. "Tell you what Hedgehog, as The Mystery of the Vandal has now been solved, I reckon the usual celebration is in order. I haven't got any left in the fridge, so why don't we go to the village shop and restock." As she spoke, she grabbed a blue padded bag from just inside the door and swung the strap over her shoulder.

Hedgehog always found the way out of Sutton's Pond much easier than getting in. So he found Pink Rabbit's comments of "Whoa, steady there!" and "I have you, so do not fret!" as he made to catch him, all incredibly annoying. It didn't take them long to cross the field and go up Green Lane, and into the main street of their North Yorkshire village of Ingleby Arncliffe.

Pink Rabbit liked the old-fashioned bell that rang as he opened the village shop door just a little bit too much. He stared up at it on the door frame as he repeatedly opened and shut the door, whilst trying to hum in tune to the clanging chimes.

"Pink Rabbit, leave it!" hissed EG.

Despite the shop just being one small room of a small cottage, it had everything you could possibly need crammed on shelves running from floor to ceiling.

A large sweet counter jam-packed with goodies stood invitingly at the back of the shop. Like a huge magnet it had the ability to pull you away from what you'd actually come in the shop for. On it were delicate Caramacs piled high; juicy raspberry Drumsticks; tubes of Sherbet Fountains standing to attention; endlessly-chewy Refresher Bars, and the biggest selection of bubble gum that you could imagine. EG stretched out her fingers, unable to resist the urge to run her fingers through her favourites: the tiny sacks of Golden Nuggets and Bazooka Joe's with puzzles inside.

And if that wasn't enough, behind the counter were shelves running up so high that you had to tip your head back to see the top. All full of large jars of yet more tantalising sweets, all jostling for space. Just looking at them made your mouth water and your eyes ache: huge round Gobstoppers that were almost impossible to fit in your mouth; fizzy, sugar-coated Kola Cubes; Flying Saucers containing clouds of soft sherbet waiting to be released; glossy jewel-like Midget Gems and oodles more.

At the back of the shop was also an opened door. A white haired, ruddy-faced man suddenly came bustling through, his round body only just fitting through the doorway.

"Will yer stop wi' tha' infernal racket! Oh it's youse!" he said looking at EG and Hedgehog.

"I'm sorry Mr Cuttlewell, my friend was just er… shutting the door." EG jerked her head at Pink Rabbit to come away from the door, who was still trying to hum the tune of the bell.

"I'll show 'im shuttin' t'door! 'Oo is yer friend then?" he asked, nodding his head in Pink Rabbit's direction.

Pink Rabbit promptly moved forward to shake hands. "Pink Rabbit, Sir."

Mr Cuttlewell quickly withdrew his hand from Pink Rabbit's and frowned, looking him up and down. "Hmm, thought yer might be."

Hedgehog was aghast. He snapped his head to Mr Cuttlewell, then back to the rabbit, then back to Mr Cuttlewell, pointing vaguely between them. Was *he* the only one who thought it seriously strange that the rabbit was pink! He'd been sure that Mr Cuttlewell, out of anyone, would have had something scathing to say.

"Pink! He's pink…" But the shopkeeper spoke over him.

"Usual?" he nodded to EG.

"Yes please."

"They're out back as we've just 'ad a *very* late delivery," he said grumpily. He returned with a small cardboard box and continued, "Got to watch everythin', as 'ave 'ad a lo' of stealin' recently. Some little toe rag's bin at it, teckin' sweets 'n' all sorts. Better not be yer new friend 'ere." He glared at Pink Rabbit who had been picking up various sweets such as Parma Violets and Fizzers, one after the other and sniffing them.

At this Pink Rabbit replied, "Indeed not, Sir. I am deeply offended that you should suggest such a thing. Quite the reverse actually."

"Quite the reverse ay? Well, wha'ever that means when it's at 'ome, yer'll be best to leave t'stock alone, unless yer payin'." Hedgehog took the packet of Love Hearts firmly from Pink Rabbit's hand and replaced it.

First giving Pink Rabbit a meaningful look, Mr Cuttlewell came round the counter to the front of the shop. He began to empty the box into a small clear-topped freezer just below the front window. Expectantly, EG followed him.

Behind her she could hear Hedgehog hissing at Pink Rabbit, "Put it back, you heard Mr Cuttlewell."

"Have the thefts been going on long Mr Cuttlewell? EG asked.

"Now le' me think, 'appen they've bin goin' on a few weeks now." He counted out six Fab ice-lollies, handing each to EG.

"And you've never seen anything suspicious?" Unzipping her blue padded cool bag, she put each Fab into a separate insulated pocket inside, then zipped it back up. She glanced over her shoulder to see Pink

Rabbit and Hedgehog still hissing at each other, slapping the back of each other's hands.

"Nope, never. But like ah said, ah'm always int shop, so don't see 'ow anyone *could* tek summat." Having put the rest of the lollies in the freezer, he walked back round the counter, stepped out the shop through the back door and threw the empty box to one side. Coming back into the shop front he continued, "Nope, eyes peeled at all times. Can't see 'ow they do it." Next, he took down a large jar from behind him and counted out twelve boiled sweets. He put them in a small paper bag, which he swung round to close the top, and without weighing them, handed them to Hedgehog, who managed to say 'Thank you' as he elbowed Pink Rabbit away. Mr Cuttlewell simply grunted in reply, then said to Pink Rabbit, "You?" After a quick glance at what Hedgehog had received, he pointed to a silver packet on the counter.

"Moon Dust, please."

EG handed over a £5 note and checked every penny of her change. Mr Cuttlewell scowled, then nodded approvingly at her.

"'Ows yer Mam and Dad?"

"Oh, er, fine," she answered without looking up.

As they walked back down the village high street, Pink Rabbit asked Hedgehog what sweets he'd got.

"Chocolate Limes. They're delicious – it's what I always have. They are lime boiled sweets, but with a chocolate surprise in the middle. Not what you'd expect just from looking at them."

Pink Rabbit looked at his own choice pensively. He then tore open the packet, glanced inside and tipped a huge mound straight into his mouth.

"Careful, Pink Rabbit!" warned EG. "You don't want to have too much of that in one go."

Pink Rabbit was clearly not an experienced Moon Dust eater. The sweet crystals exploded and crackled as soon as they hit his tongue, frothing up and filling his mouth. Huge bubbles grew from his lips like alien creatures trying to escape, whilst pink goo dribbled freely from the corners of his mouth and down his chin. The explosions caused him to giggle, which in turn led him to hop around manically. Both of which only made the frothing worse. As he continued to fizz his first word was, "Wow!" He then managed to splutter out, "I am surprised he had any left in the shop! Why is everyone not eating these? Amazing." He then carefully folded over the top of the packet. "I am going to save these – perhaps for a little 'Pink' time."

EG wiped the tears of laughter from her cheeks, "Come on let's get back to...ooh look!" she bent down and picked up a rusty old bike chain. "Excellent!"

"What would you want with that extremely dirty, old thing?" asked Pink Rabbit, screwing up his nose.

"I don't know…yet. But look it's a 7 speed, I haven't got one of those."

"Yes, excellent," agreed Pink Rabbit blandly.

As they arrived back at the shed EG flung the chain over one of the bars running across the top of the ceiling where it settled with the many other chains. One by one she took out the Fab ice-lollies and placed them in the mini fridge, each in their own special stand. The outside of the small fridge had chipped white paint and was rather battered looking. But inside was like a jewelled glitter ball. She had sprayed it with a textured silver spray, so the fridge light caught speckles of diamond-like glints in the silver. She always half-expected some church music to burst out as she opened it – 'Hallelujah! Hallelujah!' Then, taking one Fab back out of the fridge, she put the wrapper in a small silver bullet swing bin by her feet, grabbed a mirror from the top of the fridge and went back to the others outside.

"So why did you choose the Moon Dust, if you've never had it before?" Hedgehog was asking.

"Because it made me think of home."

"What, is it dusty there?"

Pink Rabbit just looked at him and shrugged. He was sitting on the ground leaning against the wooden decking. Hedgehog was standing by his usual seat. It was made from the base section of a large bowl-like wicker chair and was attached by a thick rope to the branch of one of the Three Trees, so that it hung low over the edge of the cool water of their pond. The seat was 'spine-friendly': it was densely covered in leaves and straw, allowing him to lean back with maximum comfort. But because it was only held up by a single rope and because Hedgehog had to climb onto a tree stump to reach it, there was a very particular knack to actually getting on. Clutching his bag of chocolate limes, he made to lower himself gently into his seat, a relaxed smile already spreading across his face. When suddenly, Pink Rabbit shouted,

"Watch out?!"

As a result, Hedgehog tried at the same time to get into the seat, but also to not get into it, making him to fall higgledy-piggledy headfirst onto it, legs splayed up in the air. The force of the fall then set his seat spinning round and round, gaining more and more momentum. Faster and faster.

"Oooooooohhhhhh!" shouted Hedgehog.

Without hesitation, EG leapt onto the stump and grabbed the rope, trying not to land in the pond herself. Oblivious to the twisting rope burning her hand, she heaved it to a halt. With a humpf and a pumpf, Hedgehog disentangled himself and hauled himself the right way up. Completely in disarray, he flopped back in the seat, head to foot in leaves and straw.

"What did you shout at me for?!"

"I was simply warning you to be careful so that you did not fall into the water. And it worked – you did not fall in, did you?" Pink Rabbit said calmly, with a smile, then his lips moved slightly.

"I heard that! You also said 'twice now' didn't you? What do you mean? Oh, I suppose you mean you've *saved* me twice now. Well, the first time, I was fine, I was just getting my balance. And this time *you* caused the accident!"

With a sense of finality and a scowl, Hedgehog pulled out his bag of chocolate limes, peered in the bag as if choosing the best one, carefully unwrapped it and popped it into his mouth. Instantly he felt relaxed.

Fab still in one hand, EG went back and got comfortable in her deckchair. She loved it – she had made the cover for it herself out of large squares of old denim jeans (jeans she'd found round her home, that she was sure her family didn't 'need' anymore.) It weathered well. She leant forward to adjust a small mirror on a plastic hinged frame that sat on a tree stump next to her. Satisfied that it was at the correct angle, she checked her tongue in the slightly cracked mirrored glass – yes, normal colour. She gazed adoringly at the Fab, with its dazzling ruby red strawberry base, pearly white vanilla middle section and a yummy chocolate covered top, speckled with glorious hundreds and thousands.

"I am going to require a much more suitable seating situation if I am going to be sitting here a good deal," Pink Rabbit said with a slight grimace, as he rearranged himself against the edge of the decking.

EG smiled to herself, pleased, though not really sure why, at the idea of Pink Rabbit staying around. She couldn't quite hear what Hedgehog said, as his mouth was full of chocolate lime, but she picked out the word 'joking!'. EG checked her tongue in the mirror – excellent, it was just starting to move on from being curiously mottled with various colours of the hundreds and thousands to a cool white. Pink Rabbit finally seemed to get comfy, as he'd laid his long ears over his closed eyes.

"I love celebrating," said EG looking at her Fab, anticipating the wonderful colour change of her tongue from white to red. "And I think we now have Mystery Number 2: The Mystery of the Missing Sweets and Other Items from the Village Shop.

Chapter 2

How Not To Be Clueless

With a backward kick of her foot, EG slammed the back door behind her. Her parents were getting even more annoying - if that was possible! She didn't slam the gate though – she liked the gate. It was one of those wide wooden ones, with a diagonal cross bar, which was brilliant for swinging on. She jumped on the bottom rung, setting it in motion and hopped off at the last possible moment before the latch snapped closed. Letting out one last cross grunt, she yanked her pale blue hoodie tighter round her waist and set off across the village high street to Green Lane. As she was turning into the lane, she saw a group of kids that she recognised from school. She quickened her pace, as they were well-known for being loud-mouthed and full of themselves. She wasn't scared of them, just wasn't in a hurry to encounter more annoying people.

She often wondered why Green Lane was called a lane. Really it was a wide mud and grass track; wide enough for a tractor to bump along. This first week of the summer holidays had, in her Mum's words, 'provided remarkably unusual weather' – it had been extremely sunny. Her dad had argued that it was always sunny in North Yorkshire.

The dry weather made it a lot easier getting across the fields to the pond. At the final field she checked around, as there was no public right of way through *this* field, and the farmer was never happy when people wandered across it anyway. He'd even been known to come out waving a shotgun. Not fancying a bottom full of shotgun pellets, EG sprinted down the side, loving the speed. She skidded to a halt, baseball style, pulling up in front of the arch in the dense hedge. Her favourite way into their detective headquarters. She gripped both hands round one of the hedge branches that formed the arched hole and pulled up her knees like a trapeze artist ready to swing. Then, in one smooth motion, swung both her feet forwards and through, flipping her body over and landing nimbly to face the hedge on the other side. Having made that look easy, she grabbed the handrail root and side-stepped lightly across the steep bank to the narrowest part of the brook. She released one hand, swung round to face the water and bounded across, cat-like. The first few times EG had attempted all this she'd landed in the brook at various points. She didn't mind being covered in mud, as she just lived in her two favourite old jeans (one pair on and one in the wash). What she did mind was not being successful. But having done it so many times now, she performed all these movements with the skill of a parkour athlete.

Once past Three Trees she arrived at their pond, though it was actually known as Sutton's Pond. She assumed after the Sutton family in the village - but she always decided not to think about whether they were actually on their land or not. As she approached, she could hear Hedgehog and Pink Rabbit in disagreement about something. 'Excellent,' she thought. 'The perfect test of how sound-proofed we are. I could only hear them once I got over the brook.'

"Hey you two," she called.

They both stopped mid-sentence. Pink Rabbit smiled serenely at her. Again, she felt that comfortable warmth. Hedgehog continued to glare at Pink Rabbit, but then threw her a smile too.

"So, have either of you had any thoughts then?" Never one for chit-chat, she got straight to the point.

"I have many thoughts…" began Pink Rabbit.

"About the 'mystery'," she interrupted. "I've been thinking about it all night. And I reckon this'll be a good one. A nice juicy mystery."

"I think we need to find 'clues'," said Hedgehog knowledgeably.

"That's what I thought. If we find out, for instance, what's been taken that could give us clues about the actual thief – it'll tell us what kind of person they are. We know that, and we've as good as got him, or her!" she declared excitedly.

"I am not wholly sure that it will be as simple as that. But yes, I agree, we should find out more about the villain," said Pink Rabbit.

EG unlocked the shed and rummaged around for a few minutes then came out carrying a full backpack. "Right, come on then."

"Where?" asked Hedgehog, baffled.

"The shop, of course. We need to find clues."

*****

Mr Cuttlewell tipped his head back and roared with laughter.

"Yer think you three can do a be'er job than t' police? Okay, why not? It'll be fun just ter watch. Tell yer wha', if yer manage to get the blighter who's bin thievin' from me, I'll stand yer a 'ole box of Fabs, a big bag of chocolate limes and severul packits of Moondust!"

"No! Thank you," said Pink Rabbit quickly. "I would much rather a bunch of your finest carrots."

"Couldn't 'andle the dust, ay? There's not many that can."

Pink Rabbit simply smiled in response.

EG pulled out her phone to record her questions. "How long have these thefts been going on Mr Cuttlewell?"

"Abou' three weeks, ah reckon." The shopkeeper looked a little disconcerted at being recorded and spoke rather slowly.

"Is it any particular time of day, or particular day of the week?"

"Well, ah suppose it's late afternoon cos ah notice stuff 'as gone mebee early evenin'. Ah've bin checkin' regular now. An' it 'appens on diffrunt days." He rubbed his chin. "Mind, the last few days some stuff 'as gone in the mornin's. So, 'oo knows," he added the last comment unnecessarily close to the phone's microphone.

"What kind of things have been taken?" EG continued, very focussed now.

"That's the thing! All kinds o' stuff. A bar o' soap, ball o' string, an apple, a Chewy Refresher bar, a single toilet roll, roll-on deodorant. Right weird."

As EG continued with a few more questions she asked Pink Rabbit to take photos of the 'crime scene'. She took out what looked like a basic Nikon digital camera from her backpack. But as EG pressed a sequence of buttons it was obvious that she'd at some point 'souped' it up, and that the camera could now do things that even Nikon wouldn't have thought of. Pink Rabbit held it at arms-length, sometimes upside-down, and snapped away happily, but mostly randomly. Every few moments he was dazzled by the flash and brushed back against the shelves. Mr Cuttlewell kept glowering over at him while he was answering EG's questions. Suddenly, EG, Hedgehog and Mr Cuttlewell all turned at once to the sound of the bell, above the door, ringing over and over.

Slumped in front of the door, was a dazed Pink Rabbit, his head lolling to one side and the camera still in his hand, flashing uncontrollably. The bell continued to jangle as if it was trying to escape: the door opened an inch then slammed shut repeatedly. Someone was trying, and failing, to get into the shop.

"Right, that's it!" Mr Cuttlewell bellowed, his face going red. "Out! Ah knew you lot'd be nowt bu' trouble!" He then turned to the shop door and continued in a sickly voice, "Just comin'," he called to the customer. "Ah, Mrs Helmthwaite, ah'm very sorry about tha'. We were just…er…sortin' out t'stock. Now what can ah get yer?"

As they walked back to Sutton's Pond, Pink Rabbit was still trying to master the camera. It whirred and flashed incessantly. Hedgehog finally snatched it away from him.

"All you have to do is point it and press one button!"

EG suddenly stopped and bent down, "Cool!" From the undergrowth, at the base of a hedgerow, she heaved out a tangled mass of netting.

Pink Rabbit instantly curled up his nose. "What is it about disgusting things that no-one else would dream of touching, let alone think are 'cool', that appeals to you?" He flicked his eyes towards Hedgehog as he spoke.

"People don't see the potential in things, that's all. They're so quick to chuck things away. This'll be dead useful – I don't know what for yet, but it'll be there when I need it."

The moment they arrived back at their headquarters EG headed straight for her shed. Searching noises of banging, drawers opening and closing and 'now where is it?' could be heard. Something had apparently been found as she then started drilling holes in the inside of the shed door, screwed in two odd, battered whiteboards onto the door and attached two more with hinges so that the boards opened up like a book.

"Da-dah!" she announced to her friends.

"What are they?" asked Pink Rabbit, tilting his head to one side then the other, as if this would give him a better understanding.

"They're crime scene boards – we put up all our information about the crime as we discover it. Hedgehog, can you upload the photos and print out the useful ones?" She handed him the camera.

"If there are *any* useful ones," muttered Hedgehog. In the shed, he plugged the camera into the computer and tapped away at the keyboard.

Pink Rabbit leant over his shoulder, "You are actually able use this machine then?"

"I'm not sure why you're so surprised. Anyway, it's quite easy really."

"Yeah, you picked it up quite well after a while, didn't you?" shouted EG from outside the shed, clearly quite proud of Hedgehog's accomplishments.

"I taught Hedgehog recently, so he could understand what his children were talking about."

Pink Rabbit smiled.

Hedgehog could feel the heat rise in his cheeks and tapped away at the keys more furiously. Pink Rabbit stepped away. EG called once more from outside, "Pink Rabbit can you bring out some Blu-Tack please∨"

Pink Rabbit started to look vaguely around the room. Hedgehog sighed wearily. "It's blobbed around the room, for 'easy access'." He pointed at a few lumps. As he printed off a couple of photos, Pink Rabbit pulled at the Blu-Tack. It came off in long, stringy, strips. As he pulled further, the strips began to mesh into each other, twining round his arms. Soon, from pulling at so many blobs around the shed without properly pulling off any actual lumps, Pink Rabbit began to look like a weird pink fly ensnared in a blue spider's web. With a slight panic, Pink Rabbit tried to shake off the Blu-Tack, only for it to stick more firmly to his fur. Until, exasperated, he cried,

"What is this stuff from the Devil himself? It is growing and attacking me! Taking the pinkness from my fur! Help me!"

Hedgehog moved towards him, smirking, "Have you never seen Blu-Tack before or something?" He slowly peeled the mess off the rabbit's fur.

"Frankly no. Nor do I ever wish to again!"

Hedgehog shook his head. "Here, take this to EG."

Pink Rabbit held out his palm very flat and walked gingerly outside with a tiny ball of Blu-Tack perched upon it.

"Thanks," said EG. She then took two photos of the inside of the shop from Hedgehog and stuck them onto the whiteboard and turned for more. "Is that all you've got, two photos?" She was surprised.

"There was nothing else usable," he said pointedly, glancing at Pink Rabbit.

EG strode to the computer and scrolled through the photos. There were lots of the shop and the way home, all at odd angles, and mostly blurred; some slightly fuzzy people; and even more of Pink Rabbit from very close range. Pink Rabbit just shrugged as he leant against the door frame. EG then noticed that a few were not even an actual picture of anything, but just an intense white glow. She frowned.

"What's that?"

"Probably just the flash," suggested Hedgehog.

"The flash wouldn't do that. What the...?" Without warning, the computer screen started flickering and rolling in a very bizarre way. "Quick do 'Control, Alt, Delete'!" Not bothering to wait for a response, she dived over Hedgehog, her chocolate brown hair flopping forwards, and did it herself, still talking as she did so. "Some people call Control, Alt, Delete the Three Finger Salute. It's the best way to reboot your computer if something's going wrong. It was actually originally designed by David Bradley at

IBM." As EG explained, the screen went back to normal.

Hedgehog knew better than to ask how EG knew all this. She'd probably read it on Wikipedia or some blog or in a book. She *never* stopped reading.
"What on earth happened there? Did you press anything Hedgehog, maybe accidentally?"
"No."

She turned to Pink Rabbit but he had moved back outside.

Tapping a marker pen on her chin, EG stood facing the two photos on the white board. Her rich brown eyes, still and intent.

"Right, let's think about what's been taken." The suddenness of her speech caught her friends unawares, so they quickly tried to look like they were paying attention. She played back the interview with Mr Cuttlewell on her phone, and listed the items stolen out on the whiteboard: soap, string, chewy Refresher bar, apple, toilet paper, roll-on deodorant. "What people buy, or in this case, steal, can tell us a lot about a person. For instance, buying Jelly Beans means you're indecisive – all those flavours and colours, you can't choose, so you get them all. Chewy bars, especially Refresher bars, means you're patient, because you have to chew for quite a while to get to the best bit – the sherbet. Strawberry shoelaces sweets mean-"

"You would like to be tall," interjected Pink Rabbit, casually.

"Hmm, well, maybe," answered EG.

Pink Rabbit turned slightly to Hedgehog and asked innocently, "Do you like strawberry shoelaces?"

Hedgehog opened his mouth to speak, then stopped and scowled at the rabbit. But Pink Rabbit had turned back to EG and was patiently waiting for her to continue.

"I'm not sure about the other things, they're completely random."

"Clearly someone who wishes to be clean with the soap, deodorant and, er, toilet paper. And perhaps fresh breath is achieved by use of the apple," suggested Pink Rabbit.

"Okay, I need to think about this some more," she said, and strode purposefully off to the shed. Opening a shallow drawer, she drummed her fingers on her bottom lip as she stared at the contents. "Hmm, which flavour'll work best?" In the drawer was a selection of a various flavoured muffins, each in their own little niche, and all brimming over the sides of their paper cases. "Butterscotch – no, too mellow. Marshmallow – no, too chewy, I need a quicker decision. Ah yes – ginger, all zingy. That'll get my brain in gear."

She sat cross-legged in front of the white boards, not minding the coolness of the mud beneath her. Rotating the ginger muffin carefully, she slowly bit into its overflowing edges. Then, with equal care, peeled down the case and again nibbled more muffin. Until only the circular base was left. This she lifted out, in a manner of practised ease and finished in one clean bite. EG then folded the paper case repeatedly into triangles. All this without once looking at what was in her hand - eyes staying glued to the whiteboard. She then promptly stood up and started sketching on one of the boards. Meanwhile, Hedgehog had pulled out a silver flask from his waistcoat pocket and had taken a couple of quick sips. Pink Rabbit watched them both, a slight frown across his face.

"Is that the shop?" Hedgehog asked, between mouthfuls.

"Yep. It's a floor plan."

"A plan of the floor?" Pink Rabbit asked, incredulous. "But surely the floor is just, well, somewhat flat."

EG narrowed her eyes slightly at Pink Rabbit. She wasn't sure if he was making fun of her. "It's a plan of the layout of the shop – where everything is in the shop. We need to know how this person can get in so easily without being seen."

Hedgehog added, "We need to see where the person's been and where they might have stood."

"Genius!" cried EG, raising her arms wide.

Hedgehog sat more upright, in what he thought was a dignified manner. "What? Well, yes."

"Fingerprints! We need to take fingerprints. Then we can see the exact locations the thief was in in the shop, *then* we'll be able to work out how he's committing the crimes! Simple. Why didn't I think of it earlier?!" Once more in the shed, she pulled open a deep drawer on the back wall. After a quick scrabble about she lifted out a small box. "Here we are," she said, back outside. "A finger-printing set – I got it for Christmas and I've been dying to use it properly. Mum wasn't too impressed with black dust scattered around the house – don't know why? What do you think Pink Rabbit?"

"I think *I* need a special snack. That seems to be the thing to do around here! Yes, a Pink Rabbit snack." And without further ado he turned and left.

Hedgehog and EG looked at each other.

"What was all that about?" EG asked.

"Well, he is a little…weird."

"What d'you mean?"

"You have noticed that he's pink, haven't you?"

"Yeah, course. What about it?"

"Well, that's not really normal, is it?"

"Are you saying that you don't like him because of his colour? That's not like you Hedgehog."

Hedgehog stuttered, finding it difficult to explain.

"Anyway, I hope he's back by morning cos I think Mr Cuttlewell will have calmed down by then and we can take my fingerprinting set up to the shop. There'll be loads of prints of course, but if we set a trap later, we'll have them to compare with," Her was face flushed with eagerness. "I'll just get a few things together."

All Hedgehog could do was watch after her as she walked keenly into the shed, his mouth slightly open, but silent. But surely pink *wasn't* normal…was it?

Chapter 3

Pinkness

"Why did you go off in a huff yesterday?" Hedgehog asked.

"Huff? I? I do not go off in 'huffs', as you put it."

"Okay then, where did you *go* yesterday?"

"Ah, you will see later, my little spiky friend." Pink Rabbit smiled mysteriously.

Hedgehog scowled.

EG stopped abruptly at the green wooden gate of the village shop, so suddenly that the other two bumped domino fashion into each other, and then into her. A few kids were just walking past and sniggered with great amusement. EG glowered at them. This, and the heat of the day, made her impatient with her two friends.

"Come on you two, how are we supposed to present a professional approach to Mr Cuttlewell with you two messing about like this?"

Both opened their mouth to answer, but both thought better of it. Instead, there was much straightening of spines and ears. The shop door tinkled above them as they entered; EG glared meaningfully at Pink Rabbit as he looked up at the bell. Quickly, Pink Rabbit smiled congenially at Mr Cuttlewell.

"An' what d'you three want, ay?" The shopkeeper almost growled.

EG gave him her brightest smile. "We thought we'd get started on solving the Mystery of the Missing Sweets and Other Items, and look for clues."

"You lot messin' abou' in me shop – 'appen not!"

"Yes, I understand Mr Cuttlewell that last time we were here, it wasn't your... er... normal visit."

Mr Cuttlewell just snorted.

"But we *are* very professional, I guarantee it." She nudged her friends. They quickly nodded in agreement and stood up slightly straighter. "And I promise you, nothing like, erm, last time will happen again." She again nudged the other two, who after taking a second to work out whether they should nod or shake their heads, shook their heads.

"Hmm," he began, twisting his mouth in thought. "'Appen it better not, or I'll 'ave yer guts for garters!"

"No, yes, thank you, Mr Cuttlewell."

"Now, wait outside till closin' – it's only ten minutes off. And don't go puttin' off me customers."

The time passed quite quickly. Pink Rabbit noticed EG grimace as the same kids walked past. But before he could ask why, it was time to go back inside.

Getting straight down to business, EG began carefully dusting the glass front of the sweet counter, jotting down in a specially chosen notepad, precisely where each fingerprint was found.

"Do you know," commented EG idly, "who first thought of using fingerprinting to solve crimes?" She didn't wait for an answer, seemingly happy to inform the other two whether they wanted to know or not. "It was Sir Henry Faulds. A doctor. He was Scottish. But the police didn't think much of the idea. Amazing!" As she chatted, Pink Rabbit was becoming more and more enthusiastic with his fingerprinting powder. He dabbed his thick dusting brush just a little too quickly into the pot of dust, sending up billowing black clouds of powder. And he seemed to think the point was to spread as much black powder round the shop as possible, rather than actually find any fingerprints. "It's the ridges in the fingerprint that makes all fingerprints different. That's what we'll be looking at. We use these ridges for gripping. Let's just hope the thief isn't a koala," EG laughed to herself, carefully peeling back a piece of lifting tape and examining the print. Hedgehog raised an eyebrow. "They've got pretty similar prints to humans." She hardly drew breath as she chattered away.

After he'd dusted an apple, a box of cornflakes, two slices of salami and something indescribable that he'd found on the floor, Pink Rabbit looked at the back of Hedgehog and a smile slipped across his face. He reached out and started to dust Hedgehog's bottom which was sticking out invitingly, as he was working on a shelf just above head height. With a start

Hedgehog snapped around, dropping the Gobstopper jar that he'd been just about to dust. The Pyrex jar rattled to the floor emptying itself instantly. Angrily, Hedgehog stepped forward to snatch Pink Rabbit's brush from his hand, as he did so, the large colourful Gobstopper balls rolled haphazardly under his feet.

"Er, argh!" cried Hedgehog as he scrambled to regain his balance, arms flailing around him, as if something in the air would stop him. "Help!" Pink Rabbit simply laughed, enjoying this far too much. Hedgehog continued to totter around dangerously, grabbing desperately at the shelves behind him. This, unfortunately, caused everything on the shelves to wobble precariously. A large, round tub of Sherbet Dip, the size of a paint pot, in turn, wobbled and teetered. And then, with a whoompf, fell down, straight on top of Pink Rabbit, the lid clattering at his feet.

It was now Hedgehog's turn to laugh.

"Argh! My fur! MY PINKNESS! I am......WHITE!" Pink Rabbit gasped.

It was at that moment that Mr Cuttlewell returned from the back room, feeling a little guilty about how he'd spoken to the three detectives - as they'd called themselves. Accidents do 'appen, he now thought, and they're just young'uns. So he'd decided to bring each of them, what his wife would call, a nice refreshing drink. But as he walked back into the shop, carefully carrying a tray of three tall beakers of lemonade, he found himself suddenly veering and wobbling, his feet rolling around on what felt like huge marbles. It was only later that he found out that they were Gobstoppers – his Gobstoppers, to boot!

"Ooh, err!" he exclaimed, as he frantically made to steady the tray. But there were too many Gobstoppers. He felt the tray leave his hands, rise into the air in an incredible arc and fall inevitably back down.

"Ah! I'm melting," came Pink Rabbit's now anguished cry. The lemonade had been jettisoned from the beakers and had come washing down onto Pink Rabbit. It was now reacting violently with the sherbet to create a bubbling, frothy foam. He was covered in a mass of white bubbles and looked like a sweet, sticky erupting volcano. Hedgehog couldn't help but double up with laughter.

"I am... I am melting. You must save me spiky one!" Pink Rabbit blurted out.

"Save you! I can't save you, or all the Pink Rabbits shall want sav..." But he didn't manage to finish his sentence because in that moment, jars of sweets cascaded around him, having been knocked by Pink Rabbit clamouring unnecessarily around the room. Finally, as if to add insult to injury, a full jar of pink marshmallow flumps emptied itself all over Hedgehog, piercing themselves on to his spikes.

"Ah, I'm pink!" he screamed in disgust. This made Pink Rabbit abruptly stop his cries of melting and burst out laughing. He even licked a bit of the frothy sherbet foam from his own shoulder.

"Well, well, my new pink friend. How does the pinkness feel? Are you worthy of it?" Pink Rabbit asked. It was then that they noticed EG. She was sitting, back against the ice-cream freezer, legs outstretched in front of her, covered head to trainer tip in fingerprint dust. Her two deep brown eyes peered out of a dark grey face, shocked. She'd clearly been knocked about during all the commotion. Pink Rabbit and Hedgehog, both immediately ashamed, rushed over to help her.

Meanwhile, Mr Cuttlewell, with huge effort, managed to upright his portly body, Gobstoppers still rolling and rattling around him. And he was apoplectic!

"CLEAN THIS UP!! No, second thoughts, yer'll cause more disaster. Yer'll all get back tomorrow mornin' and clean, clean... me shop windows – inside an' ou'. And yer'll do it ovver and ovver agen. ALL WEEK! NOW OUT!"

The three of them walked down through the village. EG was silent. The other two didn't even notice that she'd walked past several elastic bands that presumably the postman had discarded. Normally she would have collected each one for her now gigantic elastic band ball that she was 'growing'. Pink Rabbit kept plucking pink flumps off Hedgehog and eating them, which he claimed would top-up his own 'pinkness'.

"Will you stop that?!" Hedgehog snapped at him.

"Ah, so you like being pink," Pink Rabbit said smugly.

"No," he answered quickly. "It's just annoying and I'm perfectly capable of doing it myself."

"Yes, I can see that." As Hedgehog spun around trying to reach the ones on his back. "Yes, I am right, only the great can handle pinkness."

"What's that supposed to mean?"

EG suddenly stopped walking. "Can't you two ever stop bickering?!" she snapped. Hedgehog and Pink Rabbit stopped instantly. "We <u>need</u> to solve this crime. We need to...Just stop, ok...just stop <u>arguing</u>!" she shouted. Unable to contain her anger and afraid of what else she might say, she turned and marched off towards home, straight past a group of girls who were walking back up the village. They glared at her, she glared back, with interest.

Hedgehog turned on Pink Rabbit, "See what you did?"

"I?...I? I think you will find, oh little prickly one..."

And on they both went, as they too made their way home. If they'd have looked back, even once, they might have seen EG in her bedroom window, only half-hidden behind the curtain. Maybe they'd have noticed the sadness in her deep brown eyes as she watched her best friends. Still arguing.

Chapter 4

The Untold Dangers of Cleaning

It wasn't often that the village of Ingleby Arncliffe had a run of sunny weather like this. The sky offered up couple of white clouds, but they were so small they looked like a child had drawn them, and they did nothing to fight off the cutting sunlight or EG's grumpiness.

As a result, it was a hot and bothered EG who arrived at the village shop and was surprised to find Pink Rabbit and Hedgehog patiently waiting for her outside. They stood shoulder to shoulder, or rather, shoulder to ear and smiled broadly at her. She made no comment, but was quietly pleased that they were making an effort.

Inside the shop, Mr Cuttlewell was extremely agitated by the heat and unable to stop drivels of sweat seeping from his temples. He brusquely handed the 'detectives' all they needed: buckets, squeegees, scrapers and window cleaning spray. EG immediately took the spray as Pink Rabbit raised his hand for it.

"Right'. Make sure yer do a good job, cos ah'll be checkin' mind! Clean the glass AND the wall roun' t'glass."

The three of them stood in shock, facing the outside window, arms hanging limply by their sides. They realised they'd never noticed quite how large the window was. Or that it was perhaps the bottom of a never-been-washed wheelie bin! Layers of grime, mud and mould seemed to be ground into the glass, with splatters of paint dotted on top for good measure. And the surrounding wall was more slime than stone.

Hedgehog sighed heavily. "No wonder it's so dark in the shop."

"Indeed, Mr Cuttlewell appears to not fully understand the purpose of a window. Perhaps he considers letting in light an optional extra."

"Come on, let's get started," said EG, picking up a scraper. As the three of them worked, their conversation quickly made its way to the Mystery of the Missing Sweets and Other Items. They brainstormed ways the thief could have managed to steal without being spotted. EG gradually relaxed and warmed to her friends, as they both were trying really hard to get along. She smiled to herself, not minding so much now how hot it was.

As they made some headway with the window, clouds quietly started to gather. Small gusts of wind whooshed around them. Soap suds from the buckets were soon being wafted upwards into their faces. Hedgehog, being so short, found the wooden stepladder Mr Cuttlewell had left really helpful for reaching the higher parts of the window. He was feeling quite proud of himself for balancing so well, even in the breeze. '*Certain* people may mock my slightly less than tall size,' he thought, 'but I actually have a good sense of balance.' It was then that a large clump of bubbles flew up from Pink Rabbit's bucket straight into Hedgehog's face, causing him to wobble treacherously on his stepladder. His arms windmilled wildly round, then somehow, he managed to regain his balance and steady the ladder. 'See,' he said again to himself, 'I'm very good up ladders.' He was pleased that there'd been no sarcastic comment from the rabbit. But unfortunately, when he'd wobbled his own bucket had slopped water down below him, narrowly missing Pink Rabbit who had hopped out of the way just in time. But as he'd hopped, he landed with one foot in his own bucket! His long, furry foot was now wedged firmly in. Pink Rabbit frantically stamped his foot up and down, tottering around like Long John Silver. Catching EG's eye, Hedgehog quickly stifled his laughter and put on a concerned face.

"This is NOT a safe shop!" Pink Rabbit exclaimed. "Things happen here! He continued his frenzied attempts to free his foot.

"Come here," EG said and bent down and, with a tug, released his foot. As she stood up, she found Pink Rabbit staring at a group of children walking past, laughing.

"What?" she asked him.

"I just thought that I recognised one of them."

"Which one?" she asked, as the children turned off down a side road.

"Oh, well. They often all look the same to me anyway."

"Yeah, bullies do," she scowled.

"No, not bullies. People."

EG looked confused. However, at that moment Mr Cuttlewell tapped on the window and sternly indicated that they should get back to work.

****

The next day the three of them returned to the shop to clean the window – again. They were just deciding that cleaning an already clean window on a lovely, sunny, summer's day wouldn't actually be a bad job, when Mr Cuttlewell said, yes, they had to clean the same window, but the inside.

Inside the shop was not so good. As they put one foot over the threshold, they were met with a wall of thick and muggy air that caught them by surprise and caused them to take half a step back. After just a few minutes of the stifling heat, all three were dripping with sweat. Even Pink Rabbit's glossy fur looked distinctly matted and no-one was left in any doubt that he was not a happy bunny.

"This is not fur that should be damp! I ought to be able to maintain my sheen at all times!"

Mr Cuttlewell had insisted that the front door remain shut so that the bell would tell him if a customer had arrived. He'd glared at Pink Rabbit as if defying him to touch the door and bell ever again. Mr Cuttlewell, of course, kept the back door open so that a cool, refreshing draught swept over himself. But no further.

If the outside of the window had been disgusting, then the inside was ten times worse. It was thick with grease and had layers of aged advertising stickers, stuck fast. To make matters worse, they all had to lean over the freezer unit to reach the window. EG had to really restrain herself when she spotted a box of Fabs in the freezer – mmm, a fresh box, not yet covered in ice crystals. She could almost hear it calling her name: EG…EG…EG…

"*Carrot* cake! What on earth is that?!" asked Pink Rabbit with great surprise. "Is this real?" He pointed to a cake box in the freezer. "Can one really make a cake from carrots? Now this, makes me <u>very</u> excited indeed."

"Haven't you ever heard of carrot cake?" Hedgehog asked equally surprised. Pink Rabbit shook his head gravely.

"I am sure that if we move this freezer out a little, we can clean this ridiculous window with greater ease – a window, I might add, that has failed to look after itself." He raised an eyebrow at the window in disapproval, then started to pull the freezer towards him. Once he had created a slight gap between it and the window, he slid his body in. "There....Argh!" He jumped out instantly. "How can something so cold, also be so hot?!"

Hedgehog wiggled his long nose and sniffed the air. "You know, I'm sure I can smell chocolate limes..."

"That side of the freezer is where the heat is extracted. The machine generates heat as the-" But EG was interrupted by Hedgehog.

"What is that smell? That certainly is not chocolate limes. It's more of a...burning smell," he added, looking around frowning.

"Argh!" shouted Pink Rabbit again, losing his normal self-control. "My tail, my beautiful tail. That evil, lawless machine has burned my tail!" EG and Hedgehog leant round to see small wisps of smoke emanating from Pink Rabbit's bottom. In a flash, he yanked open the freezer and shoved his backside inside. Pink Rabbit let out a heavy sigh, as the ice-cream tubs, frozen cake boxes and ice-lollies gave his bottom instant relief. "You know, frozen carrot cake is a rather good idea – on many levels."

"What the...?! Spluttered Mr Cuttlewell, as he returned from the back room. "Get yer holy pinkness ou' of yon freezer! My customers do not want mangy, old fur on their food!"

"Mangy, old fur!" exclaimed Pink Rabbit, "I have a cotton-soft bobtail that..."

But EG and Hedgehog hauled him away before he made Mr Cuttlewell explode. That had the potential to create earthquakes, tsunamis and landslides – even in North Yorkshire.

It was now the third and final day of cleaning. Mr Cuttlewell had said even though the window was clean, (spotless more like! thought EG) they were to go over it once more. They trudged outside, buckets slopping with soapy water.

"Don't put your foot in it this time," Hedgehog said to Pink Rabbit sniggering, and nodded at the bucket.

"At least I have proper sized feet. I cannot even see yours. Do you actually have feet?" Before an argument could start properly, EG interrupted.

"You know, we should time customers as they go in and also Mr Cuttlewell out the back, and see if people have actually got time to take anything while he's not there. Look, here's Mrs Middleditch. I'll time her and Mr Cuttlewell; my watch can time several things at once and produce a graph at the end." 'What's not to love about technology?!' she thought.

As the three of them peered in the window, heads looking up and down between EG's watch and movements in the shop, the group of children they'd seen the day before, who EG had called bullies, walked past. They noticed the three friends at the window, laughed and shouted something that EG didn't quite catch. But she could tell from the way the group laughed again that it was something snide. She stood and glared at them. They didn't seem bothered and just walked on, still grinning. Except one. A smaller one at the back. He wasn't laughing. He just shuffled along behind the others; eyes glued to the ground.

Once they'd finished cleaning the (already clean) window and Mr Cuttlewell had inspected their work, he grudgingly admitted they'd done a good job. "As always!" said EG brightly. The shopkeeper simply snorted.

By this time, all three were starving, so as they passed her house on their way back to their headquarters, EG dashed in and grabbed some things for sandwiches: a packet of bread, a huge chunk of cheese, thick slices of ham, mayonnaise and a bag of pomodorino cherry tomatoes and some lemonade. EG told the other two to wait outside. Pink Rabbit had made to ask why, but Hedgehog had elbowed him and said, "Leave it."

"Breckon House," read Pink Rabbit, looking at the wrought iron sign next to the front door of EG's house. "What is a 'breckon'?"

Hedgehog considered the question for a moment then shrugged. "I've never really thought about it before. You're always asking odd questions, aren't you?"

"Sometimes questions need to be asked."

Not wanting to talk to the rabbit too much on his own, Hedgehog didn't answer.

They both stood in silence looking at EG's house. It was made up of two parts: an old, converted sandstone barn and then an additional section made of brick, giving the whole house an L shape. It had a large garden with a huge tree in the centre, which Hedgehog knew EG loved to climb to escape her family.

As they continued down Green Lane to the pond, at one point, EG lagged behind having spotted an old TV.

"Oh my crinkly carrots! What to goodness do you want with that?" Pink Rabbit asked, turning up his nose, whiskers flicking. He took an unnecessary step back as EG rubbed mud and leaves off the TV. "And why is it here anyway? Who would watch TV here?"

"People are always fly-tipping here – dumping stuff," added EG quickly, as Pink Rabbit started to ask why people tipped flies. "I love it. It's so handy – a treasure trove. And the TV will be dead useful cos it's got copper inside, which I always need. Help me carry it will you?"

Pink Rabbit promptly moved forward. "I shall carry the food for you," and took the bag from her hand.

Chapter 5

A Break-in?

Their chatter continued as they made their way up to the pond, when, without warning, EG came to a complete standstill. She didn't move a muscle. Both Pink Rabbit and Hedgehog had to stop themselves from clattering into the back of her.

"Ssh!" I think someone's here...or at least has been here," whispered EG. She pointed to a hammock that hung from a tree to the end of the shed, which was swaying gently in the breeze. "Who put that there?" she whispered again. Her mind buzzing, she wondered how anyone but them knew about their den.

"Look. What are those weird plant things, hanging from the eaves of the shed?" Hedgehog asked horrified, but he too kept his voice down.

"Those," said Pink Rabbit in a loud, indignant voice, "Those, are not 'weird plant things'! Those are beautiful, crunchy carrots, packed with vitamin C, and excellent for both teeth and gums. Something you," at this Pink Rabbit plonked down EG's bag and poked Hedgehog in the chest. "Might take heed of."

Hedgehog rubbed his teeth with the side of his finger and frowned.

"And this is *my* hammock. You both have your special seats and I felt I ought to have one too. I have my tail to consider you know. Unlike some, who seem to be deprived of a tail." He peered at Hedgehog's behind as he spoke, at which Hedgehog took a step backwards, with both hands on his bottom covering his very short tail. "Hammocks, with their string weave are perfect for tails of the highest quality." EG smiled as Pink Rabbit wiggled <u>his</u> behind as he spoke. "You may be happy with your 'nest'," Pink Rabbit waved a flippant hand at Hedgehog's leafy seat hanging over the pond.

Hedgehog drew in an indignant breath and started to retort, "It's not a
ne-!"

"But I," continued Pink Rabbit. "Have more refined requirements." And with that he marched, straight-backed over to the hanging carrots and lifted them down. He then turned to a cabinet next to the hammock, which EG realised she'd not even noticed. It seemed to stand as proudly as Pink Rabbit. It was a beautiful Art Deco style drinks cabinet made from walnut wood. "I thought I needed a few basics to make the place a little more homely," he added, as he noticed EG and Hedgehog's eyebrows arched in surprise. He lifted the lid of the cabinet. This in turn raised two mirrored stepped shelves within, containing all kinds of cocktail paraphernalia: mini umbrellas, small paper pineapples on sticks, olives and straws of all different sizes and colours. When he opened the two front doors beneath the lid, EG could see the whole inside was also shiny and mirrored, something she could truly appreciate. Pink Rabbit pulled out a perfectly polished silver cocktail shaker, followed by a mini juicer and placed them both on one of the cabinet shelves. He dropped a handful of carrots into the juicer and gave it a few winds on a dial at the side. (EG was impressed to see that it must be clockwork powered.) Hedgehog opened his mouth to say something, but Pink Rabbit chose this moment to flick the juicer on, which then whirred loudly.

Once the juicer had stopped, EG was suddenly aware that she was still holding the TV. She'd been so mesmerised. Putting it down, she went over to examine everything. She put her hand on the shelves and said 'cool' quietly, loving the shininess of it all. Pink Rabbit smiled and gently removed her hand, whipped out a cloth and gave the shelf a quick buff. That didn't bother EG: she completely respected a person's need to keep their possessions special, and shiny.

Hedgehog finally managed to get a question out. "Where did all this come from?"

"Ah, this beautiful cabinet was left to me by a friend of mine – Noel, Noel Coward."

EG whispered, "Noel Coward was an actor and he also wrote plays. My dad reckons he's really amusing. Well, *was*. He's dead now."

"No, I mean, where did you keep it all? Where's it been just before you brought it here?"

But Pink Rabbit ignored his question. "Let me get you both a carrot cocktail – you will find them positively sublime." He poured the juiced carrots into the silver cocktail shaker, pulled out a few spices from the cabinet – EG couldn't quite see what – added some crushed ice and gave the shaker a few shakes over his shoulder, accompanied by a wiggle of his tail. He gently poured the drink into three wide topped cocktail glasses. Then selected an umbrella and a small, black straw for each of them and handed them over. EG tried the cocktail very happily. Hedgehog less so: he narrowed his eyes and inspected it, gave it a good sniff, pulled a disgusted face and then, reluctantly, took a teeny, tiny sip.

"Wow, it's delicious!" EG exclaimed. Hedgehog grunted, but took several large mouthfuls and finished it off, slurping the bit at the bottom with his straw. Pink Rabbit raised his eyebrows at Hedgehog, waiting for his verdict.

"S'alright," he said. "It's not a chocolate lime, but it's alright." He slurped the dregs again.

"Well, I felt as you both had your own special things that you enjoyed as a treat – Fabs and the aforementioned chocolate limes – that I needed a 'Pink Rabbit treat'." With that, he lay back in his hammock and sipped his own carrot cocktail, his whiskers twitching contentedly.

EG put down her glass on the cocktail cabinet, then quickly picked it back up again. Pink Rabbit gestured to a small drawer containing a variety of paper coasters, each with a logo from some bar or restaurant. She then opened up the 'Crime Scene' whiteboard. She jotted down the timings relevant to the crime, based on those she'd recorded on her watch while they were doing their cleaning 'punishment'. Hedgehog, meanwhile, started to make them each a sandwich. Pink Rabbit soon wandered over.

"What are those red things?"

"Pomodorino tomatoes," EG replied. "My Mum really likes them," she added blandly.

"Pomodorino, pomodorino, pomodorino...That is a rather good word," Pink Rabbit said quietly to himself. "And they are rather nice," he added as he popped three more in his mouth.

"You are paying attention, aren't you?" EG frowned. "Oh, thanks." She said to Hedgehog, as he passed her a plate of sandwiches and tomatoes and a glass of lemonade. She took a bite, munched it quickly then continued. "Right, what do we know?" She pointed to her jottings on the board. "According to Mr Cuttlewell the items were stolen from late afternoon to early evening, so from about half past three to seven. What does this tell us?" She continued, without waiting for an answer. "Not someone who works a normal job – too early, they wouldn't have finished by 3.30. A shift worker maybe? But the timings would change as the shifts change, surely. It's when school finishes, so could be a parent or a school kid. The thefts have only been going on for three weeks – but what made them start? Could be someone who's just moved to the area or has lost their job?" EG finally drew breath and looked round at the other two. Hedgehog and Pink Rabbit both just nodded, chomping on their sandwiches. They knew when EG was on a roll!

"Let's look again at the stuff that's been taken. It all seems really random," She pointed at the list she'd made on the board. "Roll-on deodorant – is it someone smelly? Refresher chewy bar – well, children eat those rather than adults. If it was a Mars bar – then adult maybe. String. Kids don't nick string! Hang on a minute..." She turned and dashed into the shed and quickly returned. "Da dah!" She held her arms wide from her body.

The other two stared at her blankly. EG pointed down at the right front pocket of her jeans, then pulled out a ball of string. "All these things," she pointed at the list again. "Can easily be put in your pocket. So we can now eliminate people like old ladies. They always have bags, so they could nick different sized items. Old men have bags too actually – when they shop. Women don't usually have proper sized pockets, they have handbags. So again could nick anything. Men – hmm, no. So could be a man. Children – the only bags they really carry are backpacks, and they're obvious if you're trying to unzip them. So they'd put things in pockets. So, we're looking for either a man who's not old, or a child. Simple!"

Both Hedgehog and Pink Rabbit nodded. Though they were not quite sure what they were nodding at. But felt it was the right thing for the situation.

"Simple," echoed Hedgehog, hollowly.

She turned back to the crime scene board; on several photos EG started to circle, in red, where all the stolen things had come from in the shop. She then suddenly paused, hand in mid-air. She quickly looked at her watch and gasped, "Oh God, I said I'd be home by now, cos Dad's back from his work trip and Mum wants us all to have a 'lovely meal'!" EG didn't look too happy at the prospect.

She quickly put the old TV that she'd found earlier, in a box in the shed, pulled out all the elastic bands, that she'd picked up the streets, from her back pocket and wound them one by one round an elastic band ball. She then bounced the ball gently on the counter and smiled with satisfaction to herself. She'd 'grown' the ball from one single band and it was coming along nicely – it was about the size of a walnut, in its shell. She then frowned, turned, grabbed the remains of her sandwich and dashed off home, shouting hurried byes as she left.

Hedgehog, suddenly realising that he was now alone with the rabbit, got up feeling slightly embarrassed. "Right, I'll be off too then," he said. He locked all the doors and windows of the shed and scurried off.

"Of course," said Pink Rabbit. He then picked up his glass of, as yet untouched, lemonade, sniffed it, smiled with surprise and poured it into his cocktail. He took a small mouthful: "Whoa, bubbly!" and then leant back in his hammock, put his ears over his eyes and sipped his cocktail, as a relaxed smile spread gently across his face.

Chapter 6

When They All Hear A Whistle

EG always loved the early morning sunshine in the summers. It felt like the day was clear, sharp and brand new. Any yesterdays were gone and all that mattered was today. She jumped off her front gate with perfect timing. Last night's family meal had been its usual disaster. Dad turned up late; everything was over-cooked; Mum was sad and quiet. She felt the tension in her shoulders lessen the closer she got to their headquarters. She wasn't quite sure what her life would be like if it wasn't for her shed and Hedgehog, and of course, now Pink Rabbit. She quickly built a mental wall to stop her mind wandering any further down that train of thought.

As she approached Green Lane, she once again saw the group of kids that she now thought of as bullies. They were chatting and laughing amongst themselves. This time she stopped and had a proper look at them. She noticed there was one who was quiet, the same one that she'd noticed up at Cuttlewell's shop. He happened to turn and look at EG – there was something in his eyes, but she wasn't sure what. The rest of the group then turned to see what he was looking at.

"What you gawpin' at?" Shouted a girl with brown hair and a face like a Pug dog.

Even though they were a year older than her, they didn't scare her in the slightest. "Do you know what? Absolutely nothing," EG shouted back.

Pug Face frowned, puzzled, and turned to her friends. "What'd she mean by that? She windin' me up?" She made to move towards EG, who didn't back away, but a taller friend came over and seemed to remind her of something they had to do. So Pug Face went back to her friends. As the group walked off, the taller girl turned her head and gave EG threatening sneer. EG stared her out.

As she arrived at her shed, she found Pink Rabbit already lying in his hammock and crunching on a carrot. Hedgehog arrived a few moments later. Pink Rabbit waved his carrot by way of hello.

"Good morning Spiky One."

Hedgehog simply nodded – unsure if he liked being called Spiky One, but definitely not liking the way the rabbit was making himself at home.

In the shed EG unloaded a fresh batch of muffins from her backpack into her special muffin drawer. She then emptied out some other vital things from home: a couple of old skipping ropes, a rubber dingy still in its box and a deflated inner tube for an extremely large tyre. Meandering over to her crime scene board to re-examine the notes, she suddenly heard the crunch of undergrowth. She snapped her head round. There it was again. From the darkness of the copse. Snapping of twigs, scuffling of leaves. Scrunch, crunch. And it didn't sound like an animal. Her friends had clearly heard the footsteps too. Hedgehog was stock still, eyes wide, staring towards the trees. Pink Rabbit's face was serious for once, his hammock no longer swinging. EG's first thought was that the bullies had followed her, as the pond wasn't common knowledge.

Then they heard whistling. A casual, lilting sound. EG instantly relaxed – she knew that whistle anywhere. Hedgehog also sighed with relief.

Pink Rabbit looked from one to the other. "What? Who is this? We are clearly not, then, in mortal danger?"

Before he got an answer, a girl walked casually towards them, with a huge smile that touched her whole face. Light brown, tousled hair rested softly on her shoulders. Her eyes were the same rich brown as EG's, and darted around just as inquisitively. Being three years older than EG she was quite a few inches taller, and had that long-limbed look that indicated that she had still not finished growing.

"Hi, Mr Hedgehog," she beamed at him and gave him and an equally big hug, her flip-flops carelessly crunching through the undergrowth as she moved.

"Lulu! What a lovely surprise. And you know it's Hedgehog to you; I don't need the Mr with you." he returned the hug, obviously very pleased to see her.

"I know, but it suits you,"

Hedgehog stood tall as he grinned back at her. Lulu then turned to EG "Hey Jellybean, who's this? You didn't tell me there was another member of your secret agency," she smiled as she spoke.

"It's <u>not</u> a secret agency." EG scowled. "And this is Pink Rabbit. Pink Rabbit, this is my older sister, Lulu."

Lulu looked at Pink Rabbit and simply said, "Interesting."

"Lovely to meet you, at last." replied Pink Rabbit. Lulu and Pink Rabbit continued to look at each other for a moment, smiling. Hedgehog and EG both frowned, unsure as to what the look was about, and why Pink Rabbit had said 'at last'.

"He's called Pink Rabbit because he's *pink*," said Hedgehog pointedly. "He's <u>pink</u>." he repeated with even greater emphasis.

"I thought he might be," said Lulu. She shook hands with Pink Rabbit and EG definitely noticed her sister change as she touched him: more relaxed or happier – something. She wasn't sure what. But before Hedgehog could even think what Lulu had meant by this, let alone open his mouth to ask, Lulu had turned back to EG.

"Mum sent me to look for you, to remind you that you have to be back by four o'clock at the <u>latest</u> – Mum's emphasis, not mine – so you can have your bath (EG pulled a face); wash your hair (Oh God!); and get dressed <u>very</u> nicely – again her emphasis (No way!) - by six o'clock. Cos we have to be there at seven."

Hedgehog and Pink Rabbit both looked questioningly at the sisters.

"Dad's award ceremony," Lulu explained. "He's always getting some kind of award. He's a building archaeologist, which means he's like a normal archaeologist but he specialises in buildings. And apparently, he's quite good at it," she added blandly.

"Ooh, what's this?" she had just noticed the crime scene whiteboard. EG made to close the board but both Hedgehog and Pink Rabbit explained.

"Oh, a *little* thief then, is it?" Lulu said, as if it was blatantly obvious. EG snapped her head to the board, then back to her sister.

"What do you mean?"

"Well, from your photos it looks like all the things that were stolen are on low shelves," she shrugged as she pointed to each red circle. "Someone can't reach very high."

EG and Hedgehog both looked more closely.

"So it must be a child," EG said excitedly. "We said it probably was!"

"Or a <u>little</u> man," added Hedgehog. EG shook her head.

"No, no."

"Or a hedgehog," said Pink Rabbit wryly.

Hedgehog drew himself up to his full height. "A hedgehog! Hedgehogs **never** steal! It is not in our nature."

Lulu watched with great amusement. "Are they always like this?"

EG shrugged and twisted the corner of her mouth, "Yeah."

Lulu made to leave, still smiling, "Ok then, don't be late Jellybean." Pink Rabbit mouthed 'Jellybean', but Hedgehog shook his head and mouthed back 'no', telling him not to ask. He knew EG never liked to talk about personal things.

Animated by this new deduction, EG paced around, "Of course it's a child – Refresher sweets. And that's why the thefts have only just started happening in the mornings – cos it's now the school holidays."

"Yeah, I suppose it's not a really small man. Or anything else," Hedgehog added, with a pointed look over his shoulder at Pink Rabbit.

EG grabbed a marker pen and added 'child' to the crime scene notes. Then started to talk about what age the child could be, how old you'd be to go out to the shops on your own – question after question. Hedgehog and Pink Rabbit were unsure whether she was talking to them or just to herself, so they allowed her to simply stream through her ideas.

As it drew near to four o'clock, they set about locking up the shed, they waved their byes to each other and Hedgehog said, "Have fun tonight." EG just grimaced at the thought of it. He then added, "And you know, we'll have to think about what to do for your birthday." EG grimaced more – if that was possible.

Hedgehog walked off home, muttering to himself, "Does no-one see that he's *pink*?"

*   *   *

"Ow!" shouted EG.

"Well, if you ever brushed your hair yourself, it wouldn't hurt now," said her Mum, trying to get the hairbrush through EG's wet, knotty hair.

"I do brush it – when it needs it."

"Hmm."

Lulu sauntered past smelling of her strawberry body butter, her hair loose and fresh. In her hand, as usual, she clutched her phone. EG heard the almost continuous whistle coming from it, indicating some new message or photo. Her thumb would flip and scroll, followed by a burst of laughter.

Suddenly, EG's father erupted out of her parent's bedroom, his tall, full figure filling the doorway.

"Where is my iPad?! I need my notes for my speech! Have you two taken it again!" he said angrily, turning his head quickly from one daughter to the other.

"What do you mean 'again'!" snapped Lulu. "We never touch it," and she pushed past them all and stomped downstairs.

"And put that damn phone down, you need to be ready!" His thick chin wobbled slightly as he spoke.

"I <u>am</u> ready! I've been ready for twenty minutes!" She carried on downstairs without looking back, as another message whistled its arrival.

"All you have to do Dad is use the remote sensor that I made for you. It'll show you where your iPad is. I told you last time." said EG. 'Good job I went to all the effort of making that then!' she wanted to add. She grabbed her hairbrush from her Mum's hand and followed Lulu downstairs.

"Well...I can't find that thing either," snapped her dad and slammed back into his bedroom.

"Darling, you need to dry your hair," Mum called after EG.

"It'll be dry by the time we get there," she called back, without looking round.

EG's mother stood on the landing and looked from the stairs to her bedroom door, and sighed. A very heavy sigh. It was going to be another long evening.

****

"Where are they?" EG muttered to herself. The morning was one of those bright-eyed, bushy-tailed kind of ones – EG's favourite type of morning. Mornings where everything seemed possible. Though it was quite dark in their 'outbuildings', as her dad called them. Really they were old cow barns and very small ones at that. One, the one she was in now, was converted into workshop-come-dumping-ground on one side and a garage on the other. It even still had the metal railings which had separated the cows from each other as they were being were milked. (Good for somersaulting and balancing on when you wanted to be out of the house.) EG always thought her father had delusions of grandeur calling them outbuildings – as they really weren't. They were joined onto their house. The brick end of their house joined on to the 'outbuildings'. First, a really small one which contained the oil tanker and coal storage. That was the thing with living in the back and beyond – as her Mum called it – you had to have your own fuel. But Dad was always forgetting to order deliveries on time, so in the winter the house was often freezing.

This joined onto the workshop-come-dumping-ground and garage, by turning another corner – so everything was like a big U. Inside the 'U' was the garden. EG loved their house and garden as there were so many nooks and crannies to explore. But most of all she loved the workshop, despite the fact that she had gone in once in bare feet and had stood on a dead mouse! Her dad had just said 'Oh well, that's the joy of living in the country!' Yes, she loved it here – but dead animals with bare feet...No!

"Ah! Finally!" From a large, tatty, wooden box she pulled a long length of thick rope and a large piece of plastic sheeting. She shoved them into her holdall.

As soon as she arrived at their headquarters, she set to work; she was a flurry of activity, banging and cutting away inside her shed. Moments later, Pink Rabbit arrived to the cacophony of sounds. As soon as she saw him, she launched into an excited description of what she was making.

"A trap?"

"Yes, a trap. To set up in Mr Cuttlewell's shop – to catch the thief." She reached up above her head and pulled down on a rope, which lowered a long basket on a pulley. "I got the idea at Dad's ceremony thing last night. Not much else to think about." From the basket she heaved out what looked like a large net that a fishing boat would use.

"Did you enjoy your father's special evening?" interrupted Pink Rabbit, calmly watching her reach for a succession of tools that hung on the wall. He picked up each after she had finished and placed it back on the nail hooks on the wall.

"What? Oh...er...okay, dull, usual really." she answered absent-mindedly. "So, last night I was thinking a trap is what we need. All good plans need a trap! I've started to build the pressure pads – they're always fun." She reached again for the wrench that she'd just used and stopped. "Why have you put them back all jumbled up?" she asked, looking at the higgledy-piggledy tools on the wall.

"Jumbled up? I merely used the nails protruding from the wall."

"Yes, but all the nails were hammered in in a certain way so that they supported the right parts of each tool. Surely you can see that? Most of those tools will now probably fall off." She wasn't cross, just found it incredible that someone couldn't see her system.

"I do apologise," said Pink Rabbit. "You must get your superb organisational skills from your parents. You must have felt very proud to be with them last night; I am sure that they were proud to have you there."

EG bumped closed a drawer with her hip and swapped all the tools over to their rightful place.

"Yes...what?" She hadn't really heard her friend, as she was now soldering some wires together.

"Your parents, proud of you. It is not always clear to us when someone is proud of us, we can overlook this."

EG scooped up the large fishing net.

"Here, help me fold this up would you – in triangle folds, like I'm doing. I've already attached the sensor." Then she stopped, as she'd only just registered what Pink Rabbit had said. "What's all the interest in my parents? Why are you asking so much about them?" She asked with a slight frown.

Pink Rabbit merely shrugged and said, "Just chatting." Yet he held her gaze as they finished folding the net.

"Hellooo!" It was Hedgehog with a huge smile and a small grinning hedgehog trotting beside him. EG hung the net on a branch of the tree as she greeted her friend.

Pink Rabbit smiled warmly at the young hedgehog, "And who might this bundle of prickles be?"

"This is my son, Zed. He's off school today." He then added, "And yes, Hedgehogs do go to school. We are educated."

"I did not ask any such question of you. Pink Rabbits are, however, educators. We are here to teach others."

"Humpf! So you know all there is to know in the world and then 'share' this with lesser mortals do you?" His voice dripped with sarcasm.

"Yes indeed. And not just in this world."

"Yeah. Right."

As they were talking Zed had been edging his way towards EG's net contraption.

"Careful," she said gently. "It's not quite finished yet."

But as Zed made himself stop, he fell on to one of the pressure pads, setting off the remote sensor EG had attached to the fishing net. The net instantly sprang open and launched itself from the tree, landing straight over Hedgehog.

Zed scrambled to his feet to help his father.

"Sorry Dad, Sorry."

Pink Rabbit gave out a full, hearty laugh.

"You know young Zed, I think that I am going to like you."

Zed stood up from helping his father, who was almost, but not quite, out of the net. "You're very pink." He said looking at Pink Rabbit.

Pink Rabbit laughed again. "Yes, I am most definitely going to like you."

Zed grinned. Hedgehog, finally free of the net, stood up and flung it aside. He was unsure whether to be extremely pleased or extremely annoyed that Pink Rabbit already liked his son. Still chuckling to himself, Pink Rabbit stepped over to his hammock. As he did so, his long furry foot got caught in the fishing net; unable to detach his foot he instantly toppled sideways.

"Ooh! Aah!"

And, with an undistinguished splash, fell ears first into the murky pond! "My fur! My pinkness! My pinkness should not be wet!" He spluttered, as he emerged from the water. With a single bound, he leapt to dry land. And then, with a single vigorous shake of his body, and long ears, he was dry once more.

"Cool!" said Zed, eyes wide with admiration. "How did you do that?" He gave his short body a little shake as he spoke, as if to see what it might feel like.

"Yes," said Hedgehog. "How do you do that? It must be really weird fur."

"I think that I have mentioned before how special I am." He then thoughtfully ran his hand the length of one ear. "Yes, dry, but I think a little jooshing is required." He walked over to his drinks cabinet and from the back of it pulled out what looked to be a small hairdryer.

"What? You're going to use a hairdryer on your fur?" exclaimed Hedgehog.

"This is not a hairdryer, it is an ear-dryer." He then wound a small dial several times so that it was smoothly set in motion, and proceeded to 'joosh up' his ears, till they were feather-light fluffy.

"Brilliant!" enthused EG. "I like all these clockwork things you have Pink Rabbit." She then set to work gathering up the net and pressure pads. "Well, at least we know that the trap works now," she said brightly.

Zed nodded enthusiastically. Both Hedgehog and Pink Rabbit made non-committal noises. As EG made the finishing touches to the trap, Zed kept asking her what she was doing. She answered each question very patiently, as she always liked being with any of Hedgehog's children.

"I think...yes...it's finished." She looked down at her hard work with a satisfied smile. "I think this deserves a celebration." Everyone totally agreed - they were always up for a chance to celebrate! EG went into the shed and opened the battered old mini fridge. The inside sparkled and glittered like a keenly polished diamond. She took out a Fab ice-lolly, picked up her special mirror and went back out to sit in her denim deckchair. As she began her fun ritual of sucking the ice lolly and checking her tongue, Pink Rabbit made himself a cocktail. Hedgehog pulled out a small paper bag from his waistcoat pocket only to be dismayed that he only had one chocolate lime left.

EG said, "Zed, you know where I keep the stash of sweets for your brothers and sisters – go help yourself." Zed came back with a handful of brightly coloured Dolly Mixtures.

"Not those son," said Hedgehog in a deep voice.

"Why not Dad?"

"Something a bit more manly – I mean – interesting." Zed came back again, this time with one hand full of long, thin, fruit shoelaces. But still happily clutching the Dolly Mixtures in the other.

"Slughetti Dad! Want some?" laughed Zed.

Pink Rabbit looked to Hedgehog and said quietly. "Ah, <u>long</u>, <u>thin</u> fruit shoelaces. Now, what were we saying about the choice of sweets saying something about a person – maybe you <u>would</u> like some?" He kept an innocent expression.

"No thanks son, I'm happy with my chocolate lime." He scowled at the rabbit.

Once they'd finished, EG was raring to go. All four of them carried the components of the trap to the shop, though admittedly, Pink Rabbit helped a little less than the others.

Mr Cuttlewell wasn't convinced.

"You put the pressure pads round the shop. In places like on the floor in front of the sweet counter.

Put small mats on top to hide them. Then if someone's standing in one place too long - like a thief would be, if he's thinking about what he's going to take and checking the coast is clear - the timer in the pressure pad sets off a small sensor. The sensor will then remotely activate the net." EG pointed at the net.

They all looked up. EG had fastened the net the full length and breadth of the ceiling. "No matter where the thief is in the shop, he'll be caught, as the net is then released and drops down to wherever he, or she, is." EG looked triumphant.

Mr Cuttlewell now looked less dubious, and in fact was rather impressed with the science behind it.

"You have a small control box that you can keep in the back room. So, when you leave this room, you can turn on the trap and when you come back in you turn it off again. Cos you obviously don't want to trap any old customer!" EG sniggered at the prospect; her friends laughed too.

Mr Cuttlewell glared at them. They all immediately stopped laughing. EG hastily carried on, certain that the shopkeeper was remembering the little 'fiascos' she, Hedgehog and Pink Rabbit had had in the shop. "Anyway, I'll just set up the pressure pads, and here's the control box – the switches are all labelled. We'll wait well out of sight." She quickly arranged the rest of the trap, then the four of them left Mr Cuttlewell to it.

They sat on the low wall that enclosed the front of the village primary school, just a few doors down from the shop. All the kids in the village met up there and often hung around the school, so they wouldn't look odd being there. Within minutes, a huge bundle of white and grey fur loped over towards them. Two friendly eyes peered out from behind the Old English Sheepdog's long, shaggy fringe.

"Hiya Ellis!" said EG, bending down to snuggle into her mounds of fur. "Pink Rabbit, this is Ellis – she lives in the house over there." She pointed to the large family house close to her own, where a man was washing a family car with his daughter. "She's so clever. Watch. Sit Ellis. Paw Ellis." And the dog obediently sat and raised her paw, to shake hands.

Pink Rabbit turned to Ellis and made a series of clicking noises with his tongue. Ellis looked at him and barked a few times, then turned and padded away.

Hedgehog immediately asked, "What was all that about?!"

"I asked her why she lets humans treat her like a toy. She said it amuses her and she gets free board and lodging."

"Right! More like you annoyed her with your funny clicking noises, so she barked to shut you up!

EG looked embarrassed. "Did she really say that?"

"No!" said Hedgehog.

Zed looked from his father to Pink Rabbit, enjoying the exchange between them.

"Yes." said Pink Rabbit. "But I do not tell you to embarrass you – it seems she always enjoys your company. She said you always treat her with respect. I only highlight the fact that just because we cannot hear a person say something, this does not mean that they do not <u>want</u> to say it. I am sure that is the same for you and your family at home – is it not?"

Before EG could answer, they heard a banshee-like wail coming from the village shop.

"That's a woman screaming," said EG, starting to run towards the shop, her scuffed trainers barely touching the ground. "But we thought it'd be a child."

"It doesn't matter. We've got them! Come on!" panted Hedgehog, his short legs whizzing round.

As they pelted down the shop path, EG saw a boy coming out of the shop, trying hard not to run. She and the boy held each other's gaze for a few moments. She realised it was the same scrawny boy who had been hanging around with the group of bullies; she saw the same pained look in his eyes that she'd seen before. He quickly turned away from her and broke into a run.

"Dad!" shouted Zed suddenly. "That boy – I've seen him before. He's been outside our..."

His father interrupted him, now barely able to speak. "Not...now...son..."

Pink Rabbit stopped sharply. "Yes. It is indeed." Somehow agreeing with Zed. He turned to go after the boy, but hesitated when EG called urgently over her shoulder.

"Come on, Pink Rabbit, we need you." The boy looked back at him, clearly scared at seeing Pink Rabbit. Decisively, Pink Rabbit turned back and ran towards the shop. And ran a little too quickly. Straight into the back of Hedgehog. He'd stopped short in the doorway, for some reason unable to move forwards.

"Ooh! Those are sharp!" cried Pink Rabbit, looking down at his own fur to check for damage. "You need rubber tops on each of those spikes. A health and safety hazard, most definitely!" He peered over the top of Hedgehog and looked down at the floor in front of them. "Marvellous! We have caught the thief!" Both EG and Hedgehog looked back at Pink Rabbit in horror. At their feet was a stocky woman, with jet black hair all askew. Screaming and writhing inside the large net, caught like loot in a swag bag.

Mr Cuttlewell looked up, face beetroot, steam almost coming out of both ears, and said through gritted teeth. "That-is-not-the-thief! That-is-my-wife!"

"Oh? Oohhhh. And we are sure she is not also the thief?" Then seeing everyone's face, Pink Rabbit quickly said, "No, no, of course not." He bent down to try and free the still struggling Mrs Cuttlewell. But the more he helped the more she became entangled, and the more she swore. Mr Cuttlewell grabbed a limb and tried to pull her free, which only resulted in her swearing even louder.

"Please, Mrs Cuttlewell!" cried Pink Rabbit, bending his ears down, and then trying to cover EG's ears with his hands. Zed was grinning broadly, thoroughly enjoying himself. He loved learning new swear words.

EG shoved off Pink Rabbit's hands impatiently and knelt down to help the shopkeepers. Pink Rabbit's ears instantly popped back up. Mrs Cuttlewell then started to growl about 'overgrown pink fluffy things'. When Hedgehog moved forwards to help too, Pink Rabbit put out an arm to hold him back.

"I should not, Hedgy my boy – those things," and he pointed at his spikes, "they will have someone's eye out."

Hedgehog grunted but stepped back, putting out *his* arm, unnecessarily, to prevent his son from helping. EG deftly unwrapped Mrs Cuttlewell. Once free, because she was so stout, she flopped around like a fish out of water, as she attempted, and failed, to get to her feet. Both EG and her husband finally managed to get her upright. Mrs Cuttlewell brushed herself down, tried to straighten her very hair-sprayed hair, which seemed to have moved out of place as one mass, whilst saying brusquely to EG, "Thank you." She then turned to her husband. "What on earth was that net doing in the shop?!"

"They put it 'ere," and he quickly explained.

EG tried to interject with what she considered was a better scientific explanation.

"What an absolutely ludicrous idea!" exclaimed Mrs Cuttlewell. "And unsurprisingly, it didn't even work." She was still trying to work her hair back into place, unaware that her lurid red lipstick had smudged grotesquely across her face.

EG was puzzled and quietly moved to check some of the pressure pads.

Mrs Cuttlewell continued, "I was just standing here getting some crackers for Mr Myther." At which point everyone turned to see a small, very old man standing in one corner. As he wore a dark flat cap and overcoat, and was slightly in the shadows, no-one had even noticed him.

"Aye, and ar'm still waitin'," he said, disinterestedly. "One packit Jacob's Cream Crackers – s'all ar' want, if yuv finished yer goin's on."

Pink Rabbit considered the little man, much amused. Mr Cuttlewell quickly apologised, obviously embarrassed. He picked off the floor the packet of crackers that Mrs Cuttlewell had been holding, when she'd been caught by the net. He went to hand it to Mr Myther.

"Appen, ar'll be 'avin' a packit tha's not brok'n," he said, with a small tip of his head.

"Right, right." Mr Cuttlewell flustered a little. He went hastily up the ladder against the shelves and brought down a packet of Jacob's Cream crackers in pristine condition. He refused any payment from Mr Myther, who nodded his thanks. As he left, he looked Pink Rabbit up and down, and then finally gave him a short nod.

Hedgehog raised his hands slightly and grumbled to himself, "He's pink! Does no-one notice that?!"

With one hand on the door handle, Mr Myther turned, as if in afterthought. "An' thief yer talkin' 'bou', might be yon little lad come in t'shop after me." The shop door tinkled as he left.

This brought Mrs Cuttlewell back to herself. "Little boy!" she exclaimed, "There was no-one else in here."

"There was Mrs Cuttlewell," said Hedgehog politely. "We passed a boy down the path on our way in."

EG looked up, excited, realising that this meant that the trap had actually worked – it just needed a little more...precision. "Maybe he took something and was too quick for you to notice, and you stepped forward and the net came down." Her voice then started to speed up as she informed them how things might have happened. "The sensor pad should have been instantaneous, so it must be the release mechanism that-"

Mrs Cuttlewell interrupted, indignant. "I would have noticed if someone had come into my shop."

Mr Cuttlewell leant towards her slightly. "Our shop," he corrected quietly. His wife glared at him, jaw clenched.

"But we all saw him, Mrs Cuttlewell." Her friends nodded in agreement. "Is there anything missing?"

With an experienced glance around the shop, Mrs Cuttlewell said, without hesitation, "Aye! One jar of chicken and apricot baby food."

"Yes! Low shelf item. Must be the boy. Maybe if we're quick we can catch him." EG turned and pelted out of the shop, without waiting to see if her friends were coming. She knew they would.

Turning down Parklands Way, opposite the school, she slowed to a trot. Where was he? He couldn't have gone down the High Street or she would have seen him. She glanced at the three new houses being built on her left; might he be hiding in there? She examined the ground, but it was too dry to see fresh footprints. She shook her head, as her friends caught up with her.

Breathless, they were all once again back at the school, leaning against the wall.

"There's no sign of him," panted Hedgehog. "We've looked all round here. He must be long gone."

"Yeah," agreed EG, a little deflated. "I suppose he wouldn't hang around. Let's get back to headquarters."

"Ok, I can drop off Zed on the way back, Fenella will be home by now." agreed Hedgehog.

"Orrrr!" moaned Zed, bitterly disappointed. He was having brilliant fun. And he'd learnt some new swear words.

***

EG pulled open her special drawer of muffins in the shed. Hmmm, which flavour would help her think now? Banana? Too mellow. Lemon? Too snappy - this doesn't require quick action thinking. Lime? Yes. Lime and blackcurrant. Sharp, but controlled. She sat back in her denim deckchair and gently folded down the very top edge of the paper case and started to nibble round the small cake overhang. Pink Rabbit behind her, was making himself a carrot and rose smoothie at his cocktail cabinet. Hedgehog sighed comfortably in his large, wicker seat. From the inside pocket of his waistcoat, he pulled out his small silver hip flask; the metal was smooth and shiny from years of being handled. He deftly unscrewed the lid and took a long drink, and then let out another long comfortable sigh.

"What is that?" asked Pink Rabbit, eyeing it curiously.

"Just...a drink."

EG slowly bit further into the muffin. "It must be the boy. But who is he?"

"Well, I endeavoured to tell you, as we ran up the path to the shop, that I recognised him," said Pink Rabbit casually. "And I rather think that young Zed did too. Quite astute that boy. Interesting to think that he is your son."

"What?!" said both EG and Hedgehog in unison, Hedgehog almost dropping his hip flask.

"You did not seem as if you wished to listen at the time."

"Well, we were trying to see what the screaming was about! Just a little bit busy!" said Hedgehog.

"Who is he?" demanded EG. "I think I've seen him about with those bullies, but I don't really know who he is."

"Well, I do not know his name, nor where he lives."

"Pink Rabbit, please..."

Pink Rabbit looked oddly at EG's pained expression.

"Well, it was he who was vandalising Hedgehog's house," he took a sip of his carrot smoothie.

"What?!" said Hedgehog and EG together, again. Hedgehog tried to jump up, which was tricky in his wicker seat. EG looked appalled.

"What do you mean? How do you know?"

"As you recall, when we first met, I said I had met the vandal. That I had discussed his inappropriate behaviour with him and said it must cease. It was this boy. He had been throwing rocks at your tree and hitting it repeatedly with a large stick."

"But I'd thought you'd made that up," said Hedgehog. "Just to impress us. I thought it was just a coincidence that it stopped."

Pink Rabbit looked extremely affronted. "Why would you think that I should lie? I have no need to 'impress'. I simply am."

"Well, you're always going on about knowing famous people and having been to lots of places. That can't be true."

"Why on earth not?"

EG interrupted. "That settles it then. He must be the thief."

"A vandal indeed, yet this does not necessarily also make him the thief. We must not assume things about people."

"Of course he is," said Hedgehog. "Why didn't you tell me about him? I thought you were on our side!" He felt very let down by the rabbit.

Pink Rabbit didn't say anything at first. Then he looked at Hedgehog, held his gaze and simply said, "I am <u>always</u> on your side Frederich." Then he turned to his blender, switched it on and started to make another smoothie, the blender whirring loudly.

Hedgehog was stunned that (a) the rabbit had referred to him by his first name, and (b) that somehow he knew his first name! And (3) what had the rabbit meant 'he's always on my side'? Why is he always so cryptic? Seeing Hedgehog's face, EG quickly brought the conversation back to the boy.

"Right. I say we need to confront this boy."

"But he's always with his gang. Maybe they're all doing it." said Hedgehog.

Pink Rabbit popped a rather snazzy straw into his fresh smoothie. "I am not sure that it is his 'gang'"

"What do you mean?"

"Hmm. Maybe," agreed EG. "He never laughs or sneers when the rest do. And he has a kind of haunted look in his eyes. You know what, I think we need a plan to get him away from that gang." She stood up. "This requires a cunning plan. This requires an emergency muffin."

Hedgehog gasped.

EG slowly chewed her toffee and apple muffin, brow slightly furrowed, thinking of her most ingenious plan. Both Hedgehog and Pink Rabbit were snoozing gently in their respective wicker seat and hammock.

"I've got it!"

Pink Rabbit lifted one ear off an eye. EG dragged out a massive blackboard from the shed and laid it on the ground in front of the decking, so that they all could see. The board was very usable, just a bit battered around the edges. EG said she'd 'liberated' it from a skip outside a secondary school – though it wasn't quite clear how she'd got it to Sutton's Pond.

Grabbing a pot of chalk from the shed, she began rapidly sketching out a map of the village, labelling all the streets and lanes in white chalk.

"Right. This is where we've seen the boy." And she marked the places with yellow crosses. "Especially by the shop and the school. And look how many times in Green Lane." She drew repeated circles round the yellow crosses in Green Lane. "He must live near here, I reckon, or at least go this way home. This is where we capture him!" And she tapped Green Lane several times with her chalk stick, so that dust billowed up.

"Capture?" Pink Rabbit raised an eyebrow.

"Ooh yes!" agreed Hedgehog, rubbing his hands together in anticipation.

"Just to talk to him," she added quickly. "I don't know where he could live round there, and it's not exactly a short cut to East Harlsey." She glanced up in the direction of the neighbouring village. "But I thought we could hide in Green Lane somewhere and trap him."

"Well, Big Arm Tree is the obvious place," put in Hedgehog.

"Yes, that's just what I was thinking. We hide up the tree and then use your brilliant bowling skill to knock him down Hedgehog."

"Of course." He turned to Pink Rabbit and informed him proudly. "I am rather a good bowling ball.

"Oh. You are the actual ball?" Pink Rabbit was surprised. Hedgehog nodded, smiling. "How will you get up the tree?" He glanced down at Hedgehog's short legs.

"Ah, hedgehogs are actually rather good at climbing trees – a little known fact."

"Ok, so we bowl him down, then we need to trap him. Ideas?" EG looked at her two friends.

"Throw a blanket over him?" suggested Pink Rabbit.

EG frowned. "No, he looks too nimble."

"And we're not trying to warm him up! What about a big bucket?" said Hedgehog with enthusiasm.

Pink Rabbit tutted.

"Well, that's how Mrs Hedge- I mean, I trap spiders at home."

Pink Rabbit arched an eyebrow at the slip.

Then EG slapped her forehead. "Of course. The inner tube." She quickly sketched out how she saw it working, continuously pushing her chocolate brown hair out of her eyes and in doing so smudging chalk on to her cheek. Pink Rabbit moved closer to the board.

"You know, I think that might work." He picked up a piece of blue chalk and made a couple of changes to her plan. EG nodded, smiling at the additions. With a start, Pink Rabbit noticed he had blue chalk all over his hands. Alarmed, he tried to rub it off but it simply spread like a contagious disease. He began to get cross and slapped at his arms where the chalk had gravitated to.

Hedgehog smiled. "Ooh, look at your 'pinkness'." Pink Rabbit stopped abruptly, picked up a piece of pink chalk and rubbed it all over the blue patches. Once finished, he looked at Hedgehog and raised an eyebrow. Not able to help himself, Hedgehog tipped his head back and laughed.

"This looks brilliant now," said EG, pointing at the sketches on the blackboard. "Most definitely a cunning plan. I'll make a small electric pump to blow up the inner tube."

"And we should bring along a foot pump as a back-up," added Pink Rabbit, as EG gathered everything up.

Hedgehog stretched his short arms out above his head, arched his back and said that he'd better be going. Pink Rabbit eased back into his hammock. They all decided to meet at 4 o'clock, agreeing late afternoon would be a likely time for the boy to be going home for his tea. Just before tea was a perfect time to execute a genius and cunning plan.

Chapter 7

A Genius and Cunning Plan That Kind of Works

The next day EG worked all morning on building an electric pump. Pink Rabbit worked all morning on his snoozing. Despite the fact that she kept getting frustrated with the machine, which refused to work properly, she found it peaceful just having Pink Rabbit there. Even though he barely said a word.

After lunch, he got up abruptly from his hammock and said nothing more than that he must be going. While she was curious as to where he went when he wasn't with them, EG just seemed to *know* that he would always come back. So nodded and said that she'd see him later, and got back to work. The pump then, for reasons known only to itself, suddenly decided to work.

At 3.50pm, EG made her way eagerly up to Big Arm Tree, which stood grandly about half-way up Green Lane. She and Hedgehog had decided the best name for it (as trees, they agreed, were always more fun when they're named) was 'Big Arm Tree'. This was because it had an enormous branch which stood proudly out at a right-angle from the trunk, literally like a big arm outstretched. The 'arm' was an ideal place to climb onto, as it was so wide that you could sit or lie very comfortably, without any worries of falling off. And the views were a spy's delight. You were high enough to make secretive observations of certain parts of the village, yet covered enough by the smaller branches and foliage to not be spotted yourself.

EG met Hedgehog as she approached the tree. He looked flustered, but didn't seem inclined to say why. "I expect the rabbit will be late," he said. "Trundle in after all the work is done." EG began to vehemently defend Pink Rabbit but stopped short, catching the look of surprise on her friend's face. She was even surprised at herself, at her strength of feeling.

"Sorry, I must be just a bit tense."

"Don't worry, it's fine," Hedgehog. He was already feeling more at ease, now that they were about to embark on their plan.

As they arrived at their meeting place, to Hedgehog's surprise Pink Rabbit was already there – lying on the Big Arm. On seeing them, he gracefully hopped down. EG saw that he had a foot pump tucked under his arm.

"Didn't you think I could actually make an electric pump?"

"Of course I did. I think you could probably make anything that you set your mind to," he grinned. "This is just in case. We do not want to ruin a good 'cunning' plan do we?"

"Oh. Right. Ok. Hedgehog shall we practice?"

"Why not!" He walked keenly forward and checked the ground for any sharp bits of rubbish or protruding stones and strode back to EG. He then dropped to the ground and curled up into a tight ball. Without a word, EG pulled a leather baseball glove from her backpack and slipped it on. She rolled Hedgehog on to her gloved hand and pulled back her arm in a bowling motion. Together they shouted out '3, 2, 1!'. On one, EG propelled her arm forward, Hedgehog tightened his body still further and then rolled and skimmed speedily across the tufted grass. As he slowed, he came naturally to his feet in one movement with the grace of a gymnast. In fact, he was tempted to raise his arms as if expecting a score of '10', but decided instead just to be inwardly smug and satisfied.

"I am truly astonished. You roll very well. And you do not get dizzy?" asked Pink Rabbit, as Hedgehog made his way back.

Hedgehog looked proud. "No, I don't. It's a hedgehog thing – just one of our many superior qualities," he said pointedly. He and EG practised a few more times, to get the angle, speed and timing just right. They then set up all the other equipment for the trap while Pink Rabbit lolled around up in the tree. Full of excited anticipation, EG and Hedgehog clambered into the hollow at the base of the tree trunk, poised to ambush the boy. They waited. And they waited. Impatient, EG kept her binoculars glued to her eyes, scanning everywhere for their prey.

"Will you stop dropping those stupid carrot tops down here," Hedgehog snapped up at Pink Rabbit, who was casually crunching on some carrots and flicking the green top of each away when he'd finished.

"Shush," EG said to both, turning her upper body continually, with binoculars clamped to her eyes.

"And pull yourself in behind the leaves," added Hedgehog. "People can see you – you're too pink."

"Hmph! One can *never* be *too* pink!"

"Well, you are. You'll be seen."

"I have noticed you have not used your aforementioned amazing hedgehog skills to climb the tree."

"The plan just works better if I'm down here – you know that!"

"Shush," said EG urgently. "I think he's coming."

Pink Rabbit snapped to attention, withdrew behind the foliage and tossed aside the remainder of his carrot. Hedgehog curled up tightly, steeling himself for his role. A rather underfed looking boy walked up the lane towards them, forlornly kicking his feet through the divots of grass, head down. He kept flicking his mousy brown hair out of his eyes; hair that seemed as if it had been cut by someone in a hurry. EG slowly and quietly manoeuvred herself out of the hollow, rolled Hedgehog out onto her gloved hand, where he nestled into the baseball glove perfectly. The boy drew closer, absentmindedly swishing a small stick through the undergrowth. Closer. Closer. Now almost level with EG. She didn't need to look up to know Pink Rabbit would be ready. "A couple more steps," she whispered very quietly to Hedgehog. She felt him make himself even more compact. EG slowly drew back her arm. "Ok. One more step. Okay... Okay!" Then, with all her strength, she flung her arm forwards in a perfect bowling swing, aiming squarely for the boy. Hedgehog rolled slickly towards the target, with a degree of precision and speed that even surprised EG.

Caught completely unawares, the boy was hit cleanly on the ankles. He stumbled and staggered, giving out a yell of pain from the spikes. His skinny arms flung out to gain balance, causing the small stick to fly from his hand. Instantly, Pink Rabbit sprang from the branch of Big Arm Tree, ears pinned back, launching himself like a flying squirrel. He landed straight on the boy so that they both ended up spread-eagled, flat on the grass, the boy pinned firmly under Pink Rabbit. EG sprinted over, dragging the huge inner tube and clutching her battery-operated pump. The boy, by now over the initial shock, was wriggling and shouting for all he was worth. Having pinged out of his curled position, Hedgehog couldn't help but be impressed with the rabbit's strength. EG and Hedgehog tried, with difficulty, to wedge the inner tube over the boy's thrashing arms and head.

But it was too hard – he squirmed far too much. And he was surprisingly strong for a scrawny thing. The boy inched higher and higher so that Pink Rabbit's face was almost on his stomach. In a moment he'd be free.

"You must be quick! Soon all will be lost. We will have failed!" came Pink Rabbit's anguished cries.

Hedgehog plonked himself down on one of the boy's hands, so with only one arm for EG to have to battle they finally managed it. Well, they'd done part 1 and 2 of their genius and cunning plan. They'd managed to knock their target to the ground and shove a deflated inner tube over his head. If they didn't get on to part 3 quick, it would all have been pointless. The boy wasn't giving up without a fight: he struggled and wriggled and screamed.

Excited, EG now attached her electric pump to the inner tube valve. She was relishing seeing the tube expand rapidly and pin the boy's arms to his body. She flicked the switch. But nothing. She tried again. Nothing. No whirring, no air pumping.

"Retrieve the foot pump!" called out Pink Rabbit, his body moving up and down like an earth tremor, as he lay outstretched on top of the boy.

"I'll just try one more thing." She couldn't give up – she'd been so pleased with herself at having built it. She pulled the pump closer to the tube, hoping to push the wires tighter into the box. But as soon as it came closer to the heap of bodies a succession of sparks flew out at either end. Followed by a pathetic pop and a weak puff of smoke, more like a damp firework than a well-constructed piece of machinery. She was crestfallen.

In the meantime, Hedgehog came panting up to her, having been to grab the foot pump from the base of the tree.

"Come on EG, we'll hold him, Pink Rabbit can pump."

Pink Rabbit used his big feet to pump up the inner tube, merrily hopping from foot to foot on the pump's bellows. When Hedgehog shouted for him to stop, as the tube was getting a bit too tight, Pink Rabbit said brightly,

"What, feeling sorry for him now are we Hedgy?"

"No. Just don't want to actually kill him!"

The boy lay face down in the grass, arms wedged by his sides, the large tractor inner tube fully inflated. He was unable to move. With effort, EG and Pink Rabbit dragged him to his feet, Pink Rabbit grunting over-dramatically. The boy rocked and rolled as he finally got his balance.

"What yer doin'? What's goin' on?" he now managed to splutter, looking angry. Then he recognised Pink Rabbit and anger fell away to fear.

"Why did you do it?" Hedgehog shouted threateningly. "Why did you destroy my home?" The boy looked completely blank. EG put a hand on Hedgehog's arm.

"Don't worry we'll come to that." She turned to look the boy squarely in the eyes. "Have you been stealing from Cuttlewell's shop?"

He opened his mouth, then closed it. Then said sullenly, "No."

"We <u>know</u> you have, so there's no point in denying it," said EG fiercely. Then to her surprise, instead of hearing flat denials again, she saw his eyes slowly well with tears.

He said quietly, "They made me."

"What? Who?" She frowned.

"Those bullies. You've seen 'em. They take mi lunch money off me and say they'll give it back if I nick somethin', anythin' from the shop. I need that money – it's the only meal I get all day. I don't want to nick nuthin. Then they don't even always give me mi money back."

EG stared at him. She hadn't been expecting this. Hedgehog stepped forward.

"And what about my house?"

"I don't even know what yer talkin about!" Hedgehog looked furious and explained.

"Oh!" exclaimed the trapped boy. "I didn't even know it was someone's house, till 'e said," nodding towards Pink Rabbit, with a slightly wary glance. Pink Rabbit raised an eyebrow and looked at Hedgehog with an 'I-told-you-so' look. Hedgehog refused to look back at him.

"I was tryin' to find somewhere no-one could see me get angry – I chucked stones, whacked trees with branches." Hedgehog winced. "But I didn't know. I'm dead sorry."

"Why not tell your parents?" EG asked. The boy gave a bitter snort.

"Yeah, right. They wouldn't care. They'd just 'ave a go at me for gettin' bullied or for losing mi money."

Only now did EG notice the boy's arms, which were just visible as his sleeves had been pulled up by the tube. She saw the mottled blues, greens and browns of bruises that looked both old and fresh.

"Did the bullies do that?" she nodded at his arms.

He paused for a minute then said, "Yes." But he didn't sound convincing.

"Why didn't you tell someone else?"

"They're girls! How embarrassing would that be?!"

EG's eyes were flaring. "We've got to do something about those bullies!"

Pink Rabbit looked at her proudly. All the time that the boy had been explaining, the anger had gradually slipped from Hedgehog's face and now he looked pitifully at the boy. He nodded in agreement with EG, he then turned his back on the boy and started to walk backwards towards him in a very determined way.

EG, suddenly realising what he was going to do, shouted, "NO!" She wanted to keep the inner tube. But too late. Pop, pop, pop! Hedgehog's spikes instantly punctured the tube. But the unexpected force from the releasing air caused the inner tube to bounce and shoot all over the ground, with the boy still stuck inside.

It took some time to rescue their prisoner-turned-friend. Time that rather entertained Pink Rabbit.

Chapter 8

Where Pond Becomes P.O.N.D.

"One more mystery solved," said Hedgehog, taking a satisfied slug from his hip flask.

The three friends were sitting in their favourite seats, mulling over the events of the previous day.

"But it's not completely solved!" exclaimed EG, emphatically.

"What do you mean?" Hedgehog paused, the rim of his silver flask almost to his lips.

"The bullies – we have to sort them out."

"Is that our job? Shouldn't we just report them to the police?"

"The police won't take any notice of us. *We* have to stop the bullies – or they'll just find someone else to pick on."

"Well, I suppose..."

EG sat up straight. "No, we have to." There was an edge to her voice. "Someone can't be controlled by bullies, by someone else. It would be horrible to feel that alone, so worthless that someone can do what they want with you."

Pink Rabbit gave EG a curious look. Hedgehog was surprised by EG's strength of feeling. Oblivious and barely even looking at her friends, she carried on,

"Who'd want to feel that lonely, that…abandoned?" She now turned to face them, her dark eyes flickering intensely, like warning flames.

They all held the silence for a few moments, which was finally broken by Pink Rabbit. "Where is the boy anyway?"

"Joey? He's with Fenella." Hedgehog explained how Joey had apologised again to him and had offered to mend anything he'd broken, and that Fenella was now fussing over him and feeding him up. Hedgehog rolled his eyes at this last bit, but really he was always very proud of his wife. "You know," he continued, "if we're going to keep solving these mysteries, we're going to have to give ourselves a name."

A huge grin flew across EG's face. She loved the idea.

"What? Like, 'The Mystery Solvers'?" asked Pink Rabbit.

"Well, I thought something a bit more imaginative than that."

EG stood up and started pacing around. "We definitely need a name. Something that's about us, and maybe where we are, but obviously without actually telling anyone exactly where we are," she added quickly.

"What about *The Three Ponderers*, like The Three Musketeers - we're based at Sutton's Pond, and we're really good thinkers," suggested Hedgehog.

Pink Rabbit scoffed. "I like the one for all, and all for one thing, but 'Ponderers', it is a little-"

"What?"

Well, erm…, what about *Perfectly Pink Solutions*?"

"Yeah, right. Like we're going to have 'pink' in the name."

"Well, my dear Watson, you think of-"

"Brilliant!" interrupted EG. Pink Rabbit beamed. Hedgehog looked incredulous.

"What?! You can't seriously like his idea with *pink* in it?"

"No, not that. Pink Rabbit called you Watson, as in Dr Watson from Sherlock Holmes. Sherlock Holmes was always using '*p*owers *o*f *n*atural *d*eduction'." She emphasised the first letter of each word as she spoke. Then summarised: "P.O.N.D! I mean he was the greatest detective ever and was really into working out mysteries just by thinking about them. Fits perfectly." She paused. "What do you think? P.O.N.D. Agents? P.O.N.D. Detectives? Or, er..Crime Solvers of P.O.N.D.?"

"'P.O.N.D. Detective Agency' tells people what we do," said Hedgehog.

The other two nodded thoughtfully.

"Perhaps we could have a P.O.N.D. Agent outfit or uniform," suggested Pink Rabbit eagerly. "Ooh, or maybe a *cape*. We would look wonderful in capes."

EG and Hedgehog looked at Pink Rabbit, and then at each other. Considered the image of the three of them striding around the village with capes, all emblazoned with P.O.N.D. Detective Agency logos on the back. Then quietly decided no, not a good idea.

EG rummaged around in the shed for a small piece of wood and a tin of paint. In bold black letters she painted the name of their services 'P.O.N.D. Detective Agency' and then hammered the wood up on the outside of the shed door. She stood back to admire it. The three friends beamed at each other. It was now official!

"We should have a motto or a pledge," suggested EG.

"Yes, like a Pledge of Allegiance where you promise to honour and be loyal," began Hedgehog enthusiastically, then trailed off. "to each other…" He looked at the rabbit.

"I'll draft one up and see what you both think," she said.

"I think it would be jolly nice for you to pledge allegiance to me," said Pink Rabbit to Hedgehog. "Though I have saved you now on more than one occasion, so you are somewhat indebted to me already."

Hedgehog rolled his eyes.

"You know, we ought go and see Mr Cuttlewell," said EG. "And let him know we've found out who was stealing from the shop. I only hope he doesn't call the police." Her brow knitted in concern as she spoke.

"Let's stop the thefts first – let's catch those bullies and put a stop to everything," said Hedgehog.

EG smiled – she knew she could count on her friends.

"Excellent! Another trap!"

"But not the rubber ring!" said Hedgehog.

"I still don't know why the electric pump didn't work," she twisted her mouth in thought.

Pink Rabbit spoke, "A lot of consideration will be required for this plan, therefore let us think first about plans for your birthday tomorrow!"

Hedgehog agreed. But couldn't bring himself to tell the rabbit that that was a good idea.

EG narrowed her eyes at Pink Rabbit. "How do you know it's my birthday tomorrow?"

"You informed me," he smiled, straightening his whiskers.

EG looked doubtful. She never talked about her birthday. She never liked being made a fuss over. And anyway, having a birthday in August, in the holidays, always made it seem like an afterthought for people.

"Yes, when we were cleaning the window at the shop. I am sure that you mentioned it."

EG was still dubious; yet Pink Rabbit did have a way of drawing things out of her that no-one else could.

"Fenella wants you to come over and have, what she's calling a tea-party, at our house." Hedgehog said to EG.

Pink Rabbit sat up. "Ooh, a party at Hedgy's house. Well, I am most certainly up for that!"

Hedgehog looked nervous. "Well, it was just for EG. But I *suppose* you could come. But," he added hurriedly, as the rabbit stood up and started to bounce on the spot excitedly, "it'll be a 'quiet affair', not your kind of thing probably."

"On the contrary, I LOVE 'quiet affairs'!"

Hedgehog muttered something that no-one quite heard.

"If I have to celebrate my birthday," began EG slowly, then seeing Hedgehog's concerned face, continued quickly. "I couldn't think of anywhere better to celebrate it than at your house." Hedgehog beamed. "Pink Rabbit is invited too isn't he? All for one, and one for all, and all that – he is a P.O.N.D. Agent too."

Pink Rabbit grinned eagerly at Hedgehog.

"Er…, sure, sure. Course he can come. Wouldn't – er - have it any other way. P.O.N.D. – yeah..."

CHAPTER 9

Not Such A Quiet Affair After All

EG raised her hand to the knocker made from a rich, brown acorn. She could tell it had been mended recently, for while it still had its beautiful sheen, created by numerous visiting hands, it now didn't quite sit straight on the door. However, instead of raising the knocker as on a normal door, EG knew to pull the acorn out towards her. Attached was a dull metal, concertinaed cable, like the ones used on a shower. As she pulled, she heard a huge clatter from somewhere within the house, as if someone had dropped a whole load of saucepans and their lids. The doorbell was clearly up and running.

Almost immediately the green front door at the base of an enormous acorn tree swung open and a beaming female hedgehog stood before her, reaching out to give her a huge hug.

"Happy birthday, my dear!"

"Thanks, Fenella." EG smiled back at Hedgehog's wife, who always reminded her of a poster for the women's land army in the Second World War, with her shirt tucked in tightly to her bustling skirt and sleeves rolled up ready for action.

"Come in, come in. You know you never need knock – just come right in. I've lost count of the times

115

I've told you," Fenella admonished, with a gentle twitch of her nose. She made to usher EG in, then stopped and tutted, "Oh, just a minute." She grabbed a hat from a hook behind her, quickly tied the bow beneath her chin then turned to pick up a wooden broom from behind the door. "Even this time of year there's still so many leaves". They both walked round to the back of the extremely thick tree trunk. Fenella quickly brushed away clumps of leaves from a circular patch of ground; EG bent to help with her hands. Fenella finished off by pressing the front of her large, blue, bowl-like hat - immediately a small fan popped out from a cut-out section on the front and blew the remnants away.

"I like it! That's a new one," said EG.

Fenella smiled, nonchalantly fingering the edge of the hat. "Yes, I made it only last week; I was getting so sick of these leaves."

They had now revealed a rough circle set in the ground made of the bottoms of dozens of differently coloured glass wine bottles, which had been sealed together with mud, like a large, stained glass window. Through it could be seen the hazy shadows of people below.

Back through the door, Fenella replaced her hat on its hook.

"Wow, you've got loads of hats now. Can I look inside them? They're always genius your hats."

Fenella blushed slightly. "Well, you know I just can't stop making them." EG ran her hand along the hats - row upon row of various kinds, colours and sizes, each hanging on its own hook: A cloth cap, a loose-fitting beret, a felt cloche. EG was impressed with how stylish and well-made each one was. But as she gently fingered the added 'extras' – the flowers standing proudly on stalks; the leafy tassels hanging low: and a rather odd hat with what looked like a mini dormer window on top - she was sure that they would all have some mechanical surprise inside, much like the fan.

They made their way along a curved corridor that gently descended. It was lit by torch lanterns attached to the walls. EG knew they burned from beeswax, that was delivered by a squirrel – a squirrel that she'd found surprisingly sinister. She shuddered at the memory of him and then pushed him from her mind.

The flames in the lanterns glowed honey yellow and the scent they gave off always made her hungry for a piece of toast. Fenella opened a knotty, wooden door and they entered a cosy, round sitting room which, despite its depth underground, was as light and bright as if it were outside. The main source of light was from the ceiling, where the bottoms of the glass, wine bottles, which EG and Fenella had just swept, made an extremely large, fixed window. Sunlight coursed through creating green, brown and yellow dapples of light that rippled on the walls and furniture. EG could even make out some of the bottles' imprinted writing on the walls. The other source of light was a fire glowing gently in a nook fireplace, the warmth of which seemed to wrap itself comfortingly around you and invite you to sit awhile.

"Sit down dear, Pink Rabbit's already here."

EG was surprised, as she was a bit early herself.

She looked across to see Pink Rabbit lounging in a soft, sunken armchair that had been stitched and re-patched many times. Like all the furniture it had a loved and lived in feel, with most pieces clearly being built specially for the room. It was a room you could mostly certainly relax in.

"Could not wait to get to old Hedgy's house!"

Hedgehog scowled both at the fact that the rabbit had clearly been here some time and at being called Hedgy in his own home.

"Fenella was just explaining how you and she put in a light tunnel." Pink Rabbit pointed up at the wine bottle window.

"Oh, yes…" and Fenella continued effusively, how she and EG and selected each bottle bottom and spent several days digging the hole and fixing the glass together. "I loved it. The different colours of the bottles create such a wonderful effect, don't you think? Light is made up of all the colours of the rainbow and clear glass allows all those colours through, which creates white light – or the normal light we see. But a green bottle absorbs all the colours except green, and yellow glass absorbs all the colours except yellow, and so on. So those are the colours that come through the window."

EG smiled, always impressed with Fenella's scientific knowledge.

"You know loads Mum! You should have been a scientist or something!" said Omega, her deep brown eyes full of pride.

Fenella smiled at her daughter, proudly. "Well, you know I had to leave school early or I would have liked to have done something like that…" She looked a little wistful as she spoke.

"Why *did* Grandad make you leave school early?"

It wasn't clear whether she'd heard Omega but she turned to EG and said "Maybe, if you have time, you could think of something to keep the leaves off. I'm forever sweeping them up. I'd love to help you build it of course!"

Hedgehog looked concerned that Pink Rabbit would start mocking his wife. Everyone always assumed that Fenella liked nothing better than baking cakes and looking after children, and were always surprised when they saw her getting dirty, building things or discussing new scientific ideas. But he was both taken aback and pleased to see the rabbit listening carefully and being rather complimentary.

EG asked where everyone else was.

"Iota's in bed, having a nap – I thought she'd need it before the fun of the tea-party!"

EG looked a little uncomfortable at the thought of her visit being built up like this. She really didn't like this kind of attention.

Fenella glanced at the grandmother clock that sat snugly in a corner. It had been given to her by her own grandmother, so she felt pleasantly nostalgic every time she looked at it. The tower, the main body of the clock, also had a lockable door, to which only she held the key. A key that no-one else even knew existed – and she planned for it to stay that way. "Three o'clock - the older ones are..ah!..." She was interrupted by the clatter of the front door opening and closing, and the arguing between several voices.

"He is! He's pink <u>all</u> over!"

"I don't believe you! Brown or grey, yeah, but *pink*!"

"And can't be a <u>he</u> if he's pink. Bit girly!"

A girl's indignant voice snapped, "That's so sexist Siggy!"

Fenella flustered a little and bustled to the door. Hedgehog grinned; Pink Rabbit just smiled indulgently.

"Children, our guests are here, <u>all</u> our guests." Fenella added pointedly. Four inquisitive faces appeared at the door. Zed, who of course had already met Pink Rabbit, whispered to his siblings, "See!"

A smaller boy at the back pushed his way forwards, "Let me see! Let me see!" Then, on seeing Pink Rabbit, drawled out "Coooll!!" Hedgehog's grin instantly dropped.

"Right everyone, wash your hands. Tea's about ready." Fenella then quickly popped out and returned with her youngest daughter who toddled behind her mother, rubbing her soft, furry eyes. Fenella pulled back a large heavy curtain across the back of the room to reveal a dining area. Long strips of wood were balanced on a succession of tree stumps creating a very long table, which was covered with several hand embroidered tablecloths. The stitching first appeared to be charming woodland scenes, until you looked closer, and then you saw that they were more gruesome than that, as they were actually woodland battle scenes.

"These are rather fascinating tablecloths Fenella," said Pink Rabbit, letting a corner rest carefully on his palm.

"Thank you, they tell the story of some of the great battles of Frederich's and my ancestors."

Pink Rabbit raised an eyebrow at Hedgehog, as Hedgehog got up to help Fenella and the children bring food to the table. "You both clearly had brave ancestors."

"Yes!" snapped Hedgehog. "We both did!"

The table now heaved with food: Piles of sandwiches of various fillings in huge round buns; different sized boiled eggs – some clearly from very large birds; cold meat pies; (EG knew better than to ask what the meat was. She'd seen the children snack on slugs before, so had been nervous the first time eating here. But had then decided a 'don't ask, don't worry' policy was best. So after that, everything genuinely tasted delicious.); some pink things fried in breadcrumbs – which EG silently told herself were prawns; many different salads with leaves EG had only ever seen here; and biscuits galore!

The children jostled to see who could sit next to Pink Rabbit, who pretended not to notice. He just made sure that he sat opposite EG.

"Just sit anywhere!" Hedgehog finally snapped at them all.

"But Dad," said Delta. "Pink Rabbit might not be here long, so I want to sit next to him now."

"Oh, I'm sure he'll be here ages," sighed Hedgehog.

"No, Mum says he'll be going back from where he came from when he's…"

"Just sit, please!"

Pink Rabbit looked at Fenella and frowned. She just smiled serenely and then looked back to EG.

EG noticed Pink Rabbit pondering the spread of food. She was slightly worried he might offend Fenella. Fenella seemed to have noticed too.

"Perhaps I could make you something else, Pink Rabbit. You're not used to our woodland delicacies – I should have thought."

Pink Rabbit dismissed the idea effusively. "Not at all. I was just considering where to start, as it all looks so wonderfully inviting." And with that he dived in, eating like he'd not seen food for a week! "This brings to mind the banquets I attended in

Arabia." He then proceeded to regale them with stories of his adventures in far flung countries.

Hedgehog listened in silent disbelief, at times rolling his eyes.

Fenella was enthralled. "Ooh, you met the sultan! Gosh we've never been very far at all on holiday, have we?"

"Nonsense, we went to Whitby once to stay at my cousin's!"

"But Dad, that's about an hour away. This is a whole 'nother country!"

Fenella turned to EG and asked her about her family, and in particular her mother. She got the usual, but polite, answer that they're fine. She expected this, but she always tried. Pink Rabbit's ears twitched as he listened.

It was then time for the puddings.

"Pink Rabbit I've made you a carrot cake - I thought it might be something you'd like," said Fenella, as she brought the puddings through to the table.

Pink Rabbit sat up straight. "What! A cake made of carrots. Yes, I was introduced to such a marvellous notion in the delightful village shop!"

"Well, it's got carrots in the mix."

"And it's got actual carrots on the top – so it must be a carrot cake," added Hedgehog grinning mischievously, pointing at the marzipan carrots decorating the icing. Fenella gave him a frown.

Pink Rabbit carefully picked up one of the tiny carrots. "Mmm, delicious. Just not a variety that I am familiar with." He then picked up a gigantic slice, dripping with creamy icing and crammed it in his mouth. With cake and icing smeared all round his face, he just about managed to mumble 'delicious' again. The children eagerly made to follow suit.

"Don't you dare," growled their father. Their hands hovered over the cake ready to ladle it into their mouths.

Fenella turned to EG. "I've made both your favourites – lemon meringue pie and treacle pudding. I know how you can't ever decide, so I thought you could have some of each."

EG piled both onto her plate and tucked in. She sighed with satisfaction, feeling the gentle heat of the sponge fill her mouth. 'Ahh, treacle pudding! What's not to love?! The sponge is so delicate, but still gooey. And lemon meringue pie! Crunchy, smooth, zesty and crumbly all in one – genius!' she thought. 'And why would you even *want* to choose between them?!'

On seeing the delight on EG's face, Pink Rabbit also helped himself to a large portion of each – having by now polished off two ginormous pieces of carrot cake.

"You're going to be ill," said Hedgehog, looking around at the floor, as if to check what Pink Rabbit might end up being sick on.

"Do not worry, eating like this keeps my ears straight." And his ears pinged to attention. He raised an eyebrow as he looked at Hedgehog's ears, who couldn't help feeling a little self-conscious and reluctantly put his hand to an ear. He wasn't even sure what he was checking for. Then he gave a shake of his head and took the plate of treacle pudding being offered by his wife. The children all now asked for a piece of each like EG.

"No," said Hedgehog firmly. They all whined. "It's EG's birthday and she's our guest, so she can have any pudding. And Pink Rabbit, well, he's…Just choose one or nothing!"

They all chose one pudding, ate it as quickly as they could, then had a piece of the other.

"I'm sure you're absolutely stuffed," said Fenella to EG. (Pink Rabbit rubbed his stomach and put out a bottom lip as if to say not really.) "But I have made a birthday cake." She tried not to look too pleased with herself.

"Oh, oh, thank you," EG felt uncomfortable that Fenella had gone to so much trouble.

Fenella brought the cake in from the kitchen, holding it out proudly in front of her. Hedgehog started everyone off singing 'Happy Birthday'. And shook his head as Pink Rabbit sang very loudly in a rich tenor voice, slightly ahead of the others.

EG wasn't sure at first what the cake was in the shape of. Then she realised it was a computer! It was a silver flat screen computer, with the number '11' iced on, and with all kinds of wires protruding from it, just like her own back in her shed – and all done with immaculate detail. She couldn't help beaming with pleasure. "It's brilliant Fenella!"

"Ah, wait, there's a little surprise!" Fenella pressed a small switch in her hand, which EG now realised was connected to a real wire coming out of the back of the cake. The icing screen of the computer slid sideways and a small plastic hand extended out, holding a chocolate muffin. Everybody clapped and laughed.

"<u>Absolutely</u> brilliant, Fenella!" EG said, taking the muffin.

"Oh, there's more, hold on." She pressed the button again; this time the keyboard opened up like London Bridge allowing a large ship through. A small platform raised up in between, holding a plush purple box. EG peered at the lidded box. She glanced at Fenella, who nodded and smiled. Carefully she picked up the box and with equal care raised the lid. She looked in. Then looked up at Fenella and gave her a knowing smile, whilst trying to blink away the small tears that had begun to form unexpectedly. EG lifted, from the box, a tiny Fab ice-lolly! Everyone clapped and cheered again. "I had to keep the Fab from melting, so this box was the only answer." Fenella smiled and everyone agreed it was extremely clever. Pink Rabbit stood up to lean over the table to get a better look at the cake.

As Fenella spoke, the small platform suddenly snapped back down into the cake, sending out a high-pitched whine, like broken machinery accidentally in

126

reverse. Then, with a judder and a rattle, the whole cake seemed to come alive. As if possessed, the plastic hand started whizzing round and round scooping globs of creamy cake as it went, scattering them wildly around the room. A particularly large dollop landed straight onto Hedgehog's face with a splat. He fell back in his seat from the shock and then tried to wipe one eye free of the white sludge, only for a small orange carrot to follow with a disrespectful plop.

His wife desperately pressed the button in her hand, over and over – but cake was still being jettisoned around the room, now covering nearly everyone there. EG quickly reached over and grabbed as many wires as she could and yanked them out. The hand stopped instantly. The room was silent, except for one small final vibration of the hand.

Aghast, Fenella stood very still with splatters of cake all over her clothes, hair and face. EG slowly turned to her and then gave her a huge hug. "I love my cake!" Through clumps of creamy, white icing, Fenella beamed; EG had never hugged her before. She'd always hugged back if Fenella had given her a hug, but she had never given one herself.

EG sat down, not sure what had come over her. She was just so touched that anyone had gone to all this trouble. And she didn't care if it went, well… a bit haywire. She looked up to see Pink Rabbit smiling at her, with an odd look in his eyes.

"Oh my fur, my pinkness!" Everyone turned to see Hedgehog scooping cake off himself. "Oh, my pinkness is ruined…!" he said in a lilting, mocking voice.

Pink Rabbit looked at Hedgehog crossly. "I am sure that <u>you</u> could not even handle 'pinkness'. That it would be too much for you, as was clearly evident from your temporary experience with the flumps!"

Zed tried to supress a snort, while his brothers and sisters covered their mouths to hide their laughter. Then Epsilon shouted out, "Mum, can we do the present now?" And before his mother had time to answer he was off. He came back pushing in a very large box – too big for him to carry.

"Come on Epsi, hurry up!" shouted his siblings.

"We thought about what you'd like most. It's a bit unconventional, but then that's one of the things we love about you."

EG was worried about what they'd actually got her, as she had quite specific interests. And she hoped they hadn't spent a lot of money on her. But she summoned up her enthusiasm and ripped off the paper and pulled back the flaps of the huge box. She gasped. This was not what she'd been expecting. Inside was an assortment of 'useful items' rusty chains, a dented hub cap,   a deflated basketball, a collection of different sized cogs held together with a satin ribbon, and so many more goodies.

"The children have been looking for things for months. I mean it's not what I'd have chosen for you myself, but I know you love re-using old things – and well, you are amazing at it."

EG was stunned. She *loved* it. She couldn't imagine her own parents ever thinking of giving her such a perfect gift.

She looked up at all the smiling, cake-covered faces and just about managed a 'Thank you'. She felt so happy. She was so comfortable here, so much more than at home. It was the feeling she used to have in her own home, once. Not anymore.

Everyone was spurred into action and got to clearing up. As the time came to go home, Pink Rabbit quietly handed EG a small flat gift, wrapped in delicate, handmade pink paper, held together with several elastic bands.

"An interesting way to wrap a present, Pink Rabbit," she smiled.

"A bit of me and a bit of you," he smiled back. Then with a more serious face, added "As it has always been."

EG took the gift. As their hands touched, she felt that intense warmth surge through her body, as it had done when they'd first met. She almost cried out. She wanted to ask what he meant but he spoke again.

"Do not open it now. Open it at home." Then shouting byes and thank yous, (having kissed Fenella on both cheeks, causing her to blush and her husband to scowl) he bounded off.

She wanted to open the gift now, but knew, unsure how, that following Pink Rabbit's advice was always best.

Chapter 10

Agreeing Just Who is Very Vain

"Come on you two, we've got to concentrate!" EG was losing patience. It was the day after her birthday, or as her sister called it, her 'Birthday Boxing Day'. The morning sun was just warming up, taking the edge off the freshness of the day. Hedgehog and Pink Rabbit continued to bicker over something – she wasn't even sure what.

"Are you two just going to think about yourselves, or can you spare <u>any</u> time for helping someone else?!" She tapped the crime scene board as she spoke.

This brought both her friends up short.

"We said we'd help Joey, didn't we?" Her annoyance slid away when they both turned to her with suitably sheepish expressions. She knew she wasn't really that annoyed with them. Yes, it did get on her nerves a bit when they got at each other, but she knew it was because they both felt so comfortable with one another, that they felt they could say what they liked. A bit like a family really. In fact, it was her family that had sent her into this bad mood. Her Mum had tried to give her a birthday tea once she'd got back from Hedgehog's house but she'd felt so stuffed that she couldn't eat anything. On top of that her, Mum had seemed sad and distracted, and hadn't said much. Her dad was away with work, and her sister Lulu had turned up half-way through, breathlessly apologising for being late, with some vague reason. Not much of a family birthday – again.

EG put it all into a small box in the back of her brain, where she kept all the other thoughts and feelings about her family. And firmly shut the lid.

She also wanted to talk to Pink Rabbit about her birthday present, but put that to one side too – for now.

"Right, I'm thinking that we need to find the bullies' weaknesses and target them." Hedgehog and Pink Rabbit moved closer as EG started to scrawl ideas out on the crime scene boards. "They're greedy – they want things from the shop."

"It's probably more about power than greed. They wanted to control Joey, they didn't really care what he stole," said Hedgehog.

EG nodded, drew an arrow with her fat marker pen from 'greed' and wrote 'power'.

"They also seem to be very into their own appearances. Look at how they have whipped up their hair into monstrosities, and the amount of make-up they wear! Such is their over-the-top concern for outward appearances." Pink Rabbit said all this in rather a pompous voice.

Hedgehog raised his eyebrows.

Pink Rabbit did a double take at Hedgehog. "What?! I am not unduly into my outward appearance. Pinkness is a gift and needs to be treated accordingly. Once again, my dear Hedgy, you fail to understand 'Pinkness'."

"Hmm." Then he muttered, "I understand vanity and self-glorification alright."

"What else can we put on the list EG?" asked Pink Rabbit, pointedly.

"We could always ask Joey," suggested Hedgehog.

"I think if he knew their weaknesses, he'd probably already have used that knowledge to get away from them. No, it's more subtle things that people don't realise at first."

"Like what?"

Mulling over the question, EG gently tapped the marker pen on her lips then started to write as she explained her ideas. "The one with ginger hair always seems a little on the edge of the group – she's never saying much. And she's often looking at her watch, like she's got to be somewhere, like her parents said she's got to be back by a certain time."

"Which one's she again?" Asked Hedgehog.

EG scrolled swiftly through the photos on her phone and found the few usable ones that Pink Rabbit had taken when they'd come back from the village shop. Standing back, she pointed her phone at the white board. At the beginning of the summer holidays, bored one day, she had created a small projector app which allowed her to project images onto the whiteboard. Using this now, she enlarged 'Ginger One'. "See, she's staring down the road, not at the group, with a distracted look on her face. It seems like she wants to go somewhere."

The others nodded in agreement.

"I reckon if she's someone who's worried about being late home cos she'll be in trouble, or something, we can somehow use this – not sure how yet." She tapped the screen of her phone which had the photo of the bullies; Ginger One zoomed out and another face was enlarged. "Next is 'Pug Face'. Look how she's positioned herself next to the tall, broad one: 'Big One', who I think is the leader of the gang – as if by trying to stand as close as possible to Big One, she thinks she's also a powerful member of the gang."

"She does look a bit younger than the others, doesn't she?" said Hedgehog, tilting his head to get a better look at her.

"She does, yes. I hadn't noticed that. That might be useful."

"She *is* a Pug Face! Look at those pudgy cheeks and dark, squinty eyes," said Pink Rabbit. "And you have both noticed her shoes, have you not?"

Hedgehog and EG peered at the photo on the board. Both then looked a little blank.

"Look at Big Ones shoes also," said Pink Rabbit.

"Oh yes, she's got the same shoes as Big One! She's definitely trying to be in with her."

"Same shoes, just cheaper version," stated Pink Rabbit, knowledgeably. "So, you think Big One is the leader. Well, she is the tallest. Tall people are usually the leaders, and the best ones." As he spoke, he stroked his ears up tall and stood very straight backed.

"Ears do not count as height!" said Hedgehog. "Anyway, not all leaders are tall. What about Mussolini, Hitler, Stalin?"

"They were dictators – you see yourself as a dictator do you, little Spiky one? Someone who controls people?"

"No! Ok. What about Gandhi and Churchill? They weren't tall."

"Yes. I agree they were good leaders. And they only came up to here on me (he showed their heights with his hand), when we were side by side."

"You didn't know them," scorned Hedgehog.

Pink Rabbit opened his mouth to answer.

In the meantime, EG had been zooming in and out of the photo. "Look at Big One: she's tossing her hair – we saw her do that whenever we passed her. She's got the most make-up on. Probably like a mask for her. Take all that gunk off and she'd be very vulnerable, I bet."

"Like Samson. He…"

"No, you didn't know him either!" interrupted Hedgehog.

"Hmm," said EG, thoughtfully.

"What?"

She zoomed in on Big One's shoes. "If you look at her heels, she's popping out of the shoes, as if she's got some built up insole inside them." EG then tapped her phone and a ruler tool came up on the whiteboard. She measured the shoes against Pug Face's similar ones. "Look, the back of the ankle and heel seem to be about 3 or 4 cm higher. And the shoes have got fairly big heels already. You know what, I don't think she's as tall as she's trying to make out. I wonder what the others would think if she was brought down to size."

"Yes, she most certainly would be a lot smaller. Closer to Squatty's size," suggested Pink Rabbit.

Laughing at the name, EG now zoomed in on her. "Now, she's an oddity. She's so broad and square – yes very 'squat', Pink Rabbit. But incredibly long hair. Though all that blondeness must be dyed, it's so coarse looking. And see how she's standing – so girly. Probably worried being so squat someone will think she's a boy."

"A right motley crew," said Pink Rabbit. "Much like a bunch of wild pirates!"

Hedgehog laughed. "Maybe we should get them to walk the plank!" Pink Rabbit laughed in turn. Hedgehog looked at him, surprised, then laughed again.

"Hey, that's not such a bad idea," said EG, slowly.

"What?"

"We'll make them walk the plank."

"What do you mean?" asked Hedgehog. "We haven't got a pirate ship. What am I saying, there's not even any sea for miles!"

"No, but you've given me a brilliant idea." She stood up and paced around. "Yes. I think it will work. It'll be the best plan ever!" Pink Rabbit and Hedgehog look at each other, bewildered. "But maybe we'll need to test it out first." With that, she marched off to the shed and the others could hear her rummaging around inside: clatters and opening and shutting of drawers were followed by 'That's not right' or 'Oh yes, perfect'.

It was some time later and EG was still lost in her shed, when Pink Rabbit and Hedgehog agreed that when EG was like this there was no point in trying to talk to her.

Hedgehog shouted out, "Right, EG we're just going home now then." No answer came – just more clatters.

As Hedgehog and Pink Rabbit squeezed out through the hedge from their headquarters, Hedgehog, having pushed away Pink Rabbit's 'helping' hand the whole way, said, "Where do you live, anyway?"

Pink Rabbit waved a hand vaguely across the unploughed, grassy field in front of them. Hedgehog scanned the field but couldn't see anywhere likely.

"Hmm. Well, I'll just see you later then." And Hedgehog turned left to make his way back to his tree.

"Not if I see you first!"

Hedgehog turned back to retort what a stupid, childlike thing that was to say, and ask why people ever came out with it. But Pink Rabbit was already halfway across the field, hopping in huge bounds. Hedgehog marvelled at how the rabbit managed to keep his ears so straight as his bounced, and so, well, alert-looking. His hand went involuntarily to one of his own ears. He shook his head and turned for home, wondering both where Pink Rabbit really did live and what on earth was EG's 'best plan ever!'?

Chapter 11

How to Bring a Plan Together

"But, you need to have *some* breakfast," said EG's Mum. Her words were half muffled by the piece of toast that she gripped in her mouth, as she searched through her briefcase. In an almost a mirror image, EG rummaged in her backpack with her back to her mother. Without raising her head, she replied, "I haven't time."

Her mother finally looked up, torn between feeding her child and having to get to work. "I have to see this client today; I must do this presentation. You will be alright on your own, won't you?" she asked, anxiously.

"I'm alright every day, aren't I?" EG grumbled, as she too finally lifted her head to look straight at her mother.

EG's eye flickered with something that her mother couldn't quite work out. Anger? Hatred? Loneliness? Or nothing? It was hard to see behind those deep brown eyes, their richness always looking slightly mysterious. Beautiful eyes. She'd always felt mesmerised by them. Even as she stood there, the wonderful memories of holding and cuddling her youngest daughter as a baby, of just staring into them for hours were so vivid and fresh.

"Take some money and make sure you get something to eat later."

"Ok," said EG in a noncommittal way. Scooping up the money that her mother had dug out off the kitchen counter, she flung her backpack over her shoulders then picked up a large box, which she could just about get her arms around.

She started to make her way to P.O.N.D headquarters, then slowed as she realised that she <u>was</u> starving. She'd been awake half the night planning her idea and had got up early to iron out a few issues. Maybe she'd just detour down to Patterson's farm and pick up some eggs and bacon. At the mere thought, her tummy rumbled very loudly. Decision made.

She turned right, rather than left as she normally would have when she went down Green Lane. As she followed the bend into Priory Way, she saw three boys kicking a football between them while they walked down the road. Seeing EG, one, with a mop of bright blond hair, shouted,

"Hey – haven't seen you for ages. Are you coming to play? We're off to Jake's house." He flicked the ball up on his foot and started to play keepy-uppies.

"Er, sorry can't. Got to do something," she answered vaguely.

The blond boy looked at her for a moment, surprised, because EG always used to be up for a game of football. Then shrugged. She watched them continue round the corner, casually knocking the ball around, laughing at each other after a bad pass.

Once they were out of sight, she moved to a large metal gate next to a field, full of swaying wheat. As the ears of wheat stood about shoulder height she knew they were almost ready for harvest. Normally she would have simply launched herself over the gate and zig-zagged across the field, pretending she was making some kind of crop circle. This time, she paused for a moment, deciding how to negotiate the heavy backpack and awkward box. Finally, leaning right over on her stomach, over the top bar, she managed to let the box slip gently to the ground. However, as she released it, the weight of her backpack caused her to somersault forward over the gate. She just about managed to grab the gate and land without too much pain, but she did have to check round to make sure no-one had seen her looking stupid! She dragged the box over to the near corner, where there was a small but dense hedgerow – which she referred to as her 'Safety Hedge'. Named because she knew she could hide anything in it for days and it would be safe from anyone and anything. Having secreted her box and bag inside, she ran down the field, arms outstretched, letting the knuckles of wheat whip through her fingers. Through a succession of small fields, she came to the bottom village, Ingleby Cross.

EG knocked and waited at the farm door, peering round. Farms were always interesting places. Old Mrs Patterson shuffled to the door in mud spattered wellies. "Oh, it's you, is it? Come for yer eggs?" she asked, pushing her white hair out of her eyes with the back of her hand.

"No, yes, well not the normal order. Can I have three eggs and three rashers of bacon please?"

"Hmm, odd amount. But s'pose."

EG ran easily back up the fields, found her stash in the Safety Hedge and still arrived early at P.O.N.D. She was just cooking everything over a camping stove when both Pink Rabbit and Hedgehog arrived.

"So, I saw you first!"

"For the last time," said Hedgehog. "No you didn't. Look it doesn't even matter anyway, it's just a thing people say, 'Not if I see you first'."

Pink Rabbit just smiled knowingly, which only annoyed Hedgehog more.

They both stopped short at the rich smell of fried bacon and eggs sizzling and crackling in the pan. Both their noses twitched as the aromas wafted around them, like invisible snakes caressing and drawing them in.

"Want some?"

Hedgehog, unable to resist, patted his stomach. "Well, I've had *some* breakfast this morning, but I'm sure I could squeeze in a bit more."

As Pink Rabbit dunked a carrot into his runny egg yolk, his whiskers flickering in a rather satisfied manner, Hedgehog asked "So, what was all that rummaging yesterday and what with the pirates and the plank?"

EG put her plate to one side and carefully lifted something out of the large box she had brought with her. It was a model of the inside of a water tower. There were planks (made from Fab ice-lolly sticks) over a baking tray 'tank' of water; a thin tube from the bottom of a joke flower (that normally squirted water) lay around the tank and several small wind-up toys bobbed up and down in the water. Perched round the tank was a surreal collection of grubby, broken dolls with cut-out photos of the bullies on each doll. EG had also made some Play-Doh figures to represent the three of them. Hedgehog was not too happy with his, as it was a bit round. Pink Rabbit laughed until he saw his own. It was orange!

"Well, I didn't have much Play-Doh left."

"Yes, but orange? What a ridiculous colour!"

EG ignored him and started to explain. She demonstrated the pump, the wind-up toys and all the details of her model, at times pointing to relevant sections of a drawn plan on a large scroll of paper. Hedgehog and Pink Rabbit offered an 'Hmm' or an 'Oh right' in what they considered were appropriate places. Finally EG looked up, apprehensive as to what they were thinking of her plan.

"I love it!" exclaimed Hedgehog.

"If he loves it, then so do I," said Pink Rabbit. Hedgehog gave him a sideways scowl. Pink Rabbit simply smiled.

"I really love the idea of fake piranhas. I can't wait to see the look on the bullies' faces," added Hedgehog.

"Ooh, the spikes are out today, oh little leaf collector." And Pink Rabbit pretended to touch and hurt himself on one of Hedgehog's spines. "Actually, I do have one question. What is this tower of water that you keep referring to? Is it like a tsunami? I can see it is important."

Hedgehog spluttered, "Er, yes, just a bit important to the whole plan!"

"The village water tower is a small building that used to supply water to the village, but now stores water for emergencies. Obviously the plan will become much clearer once we get started," said EG.

"We'll need to start soon, I can't stand thinking of Joey still scared of those…girls," Hedgehog shook his head, anger rising.

"Well, today is Friday and they never seem to be about at the weekend, no doubt off shopping or something. They're bound to be out Monday – we'll do it then."

"That only gives us two days to get ready," said Pink Rabbit.

EG stood up. "Plenty of time! We'll be like the A Team!"

"Who?" But EG was already in the shed dragging out various items she knew they'd need.

Hedgehog answered for her, "Oh, she always says that. She says it's from an old TV programme that she loves. Don't know it myself but she sometimes calls me Mr T. I always assume he's a brave character from the programme. Brave; maybe strong. I'm sure really good looking."

"Hmmm. I wonder if there is one that I could be?" Pink Rabbit mused, stroking his whiskers to the very tips.

EG appeared from the back of the shed lugging large pieces of wood that she kept there under a huge tarpaulin.

"EG, who could I be?"

"Huh?" she was staring at the collection of wood, thinking.

"In this A Team."

She looked at him and considered. 'Face'. No, 'Murdoch'. Both.

"Are either of them Pink?"

"No."

"Rabbits?"

"One maybe sometimes thinks he is."

"I will be that one. A great mind clearly, if he thinks he could be a rabbit."

"OK, you're Murdoch."

Pink Rabbit looked pleased with himself. "Who are you EG?"

"Oh she's always Hannibal – the brains of the outfit."

"Oh, ok. Well, it is your team."

"Thanks," said EG with a hint of sarcasm. "Tell you what, once we've finished for today, I'll play an A Team episode on the computer, see what you think. It was one of my dad's favourites when he was little, so he got me into it. We used to watch it together, just me and him. He doesn't have time now." Her voice trailed off as she finished. Realising she'd said more about herself than she'd intended, she quickly added, "Come on Pink Rabbit, get a saw and cut these bits of wood – the measurements are on the plan."

Pink Rabbit gave her a warm smile, seemingly pleased about something, then set to work. EG and Hedgehog looked at each other, surprised to see him measure, mark and saw the wood like a real professional. He had even propped a pencil behind one ear.

"How come you're so good at this?" asked EG.

Without stopping, and rather airily, he replied, "Oh, I had a friend who was a carpenter once."

EG carried on with her own tasks as Hedgehog asked this friend's name, just to make conversation.

"Jesus."

Hedgehog blew out heavily. "You did NOT know Jesus!"

"I did not say which Jesus…" He smiled cheekily.

Hedgehog rolled his eyes.

146

They agreed that the best time to take all the equipment up to the village water tower was when it got dark. It was far too much to take in broad daylight without arousing suspicion, especially since you weren't actually allowed in the water tower. Though not being allowed in had obviously never stopped EG before. They would then spend the Sunday setting everything up.

After several hours of sawing, drilling and Gaffa taping, EG finally said, "That's everything, I think. Let's watch the A Team now. The best bits are their 'plans."

They all decided it was also a cause for celebration, the fact that their plan was now 'coming together'. As EG went into the shed, Pink Rabbit quietly followed her.

"Did you like my birthday gift to you?" he asked.

EG jumped slightly, as she hadn't heard him come in. She picked it off the shelf. "Yes, yes. Course. I meant to say, sorry. But, does it mean…something?" She held up a stunningly rich, black, swing mirror, with words etched at the bottom of the glass: *Truly See Yourself. See yourself As The World Sees You.*

"It is a new Fab mirror. I noticed that your old one was a little cracked. This one is made of ebony, which, like many of the best things, will last for ever. I also wanted you to consider how all your loved ones see you. Maybe you think they see a different EG. They do not. We all see 'you'.

She opened her mouth to speak but he had already bounded off. She looked down at the beautiful, rectangular mirror. She knew ebony was a really dense, black wood from places like Africa and India. But she also knew that the trees were protected in most countries, so she wondered where Pink Rabbit had got it from.

Still pondering, she picked up one of her laptops, one that had a really large screen, and set it and her beautiful new mirror up outside. She returned to her mini fridge for her Fab lolly. The beauty of the interior of the fridge never ceased to delight her. Sides speckled with sparkly paint, reflecting light like a thousand mirrors. She then felt the pop of an exciting thought: 'What would it look like with a different coloured light bulb?!' After rummaging in a drawer and unable to find one that would fit, she considered a possible solution – but there was no time now. These things needed to be done properly. So she made a note for herself on her blackboard. Through the thrum of Pink Rabbit's blender, she could hear Hedgehog shouting for her to hurry up.

Pink Rabbit had just opened his drinks cabinet and was deliberating over his choice of spices to add today. He ran his fingers along the tops of the small, cut glass jars, all in neat rows on the inside of the doors. "Ginger, I think, a bit of a kick for tomorrow. Actually, fresh ginger would be better, but I have no fridge to store fresh ingredients." He turned round. "Maybe I need a carrot fridge."

"Or a 'Carrot Cooler,'" suggested Hedgehog.

"Now that, my Hedgy one, is well thought up."

Hedgehog tried not to look too pleased at receiving a compliment from Pink Rabbit; he then felt annoyed at himself that he was at all bothered about what the rabbit thought of him.

Plucking some cocktail decorations from a silver box, Pink Rabbit arranged them artistically in his glass. He then stepped nimbly into his hammock, drink in hand.

In the meantime, Hedgehog had already cosied himself into his seat and had begun sucking on a chocolate lime. He peered into his paper bag to see how many remained and then wriggled slightly to pull out his hip flask from his waistcoat pocket.

Pink Rabbit watched silently, then said, "Enjoying your Woodland Wine?"

Hedgehog shrugged and smiled, still not disclosing exactly what was in the flask.

EG adjusted the laptop at an angle so that they could all see the screen from where they sat. She clicked play, sat back in her denim deckchair and quickly glanced at her tongue in the mirror – already multi-coloured from the sprinkles. A little flash of her Mum, cross at her for having these artificial colours, made her feel slightly guilty. The image was then replaced with her Mum dashing off this morning, as usual, so her guilt disappeared. As the credits rolled on the screen for the start of the A Team, a smile spread across her face – she'd chosen one of her favourite episodes. However, her contentment was quickly broken by a surprised shout from Pink Rabbit.

"*You* are Mr T?!"

Hedgehog looked smug and proud.

"This huge beef of a man? With ginormous muscles and a Mohican hair- cut? With an unseemly amount of tacky, gold chains around his neck?"

Hedgehog's smugness started to waiver. "Yes, he is suitably strong and brave."

"You are *not* Mr T!"

Hedgehog scowled. "I am. Anyway, it's not up to you, EG gets to choose."

Pink Rabbit made a spluttering noise at such a feeble argument. He turned back to the screen and watched a little more. "Hmm, maybe actually. He is not very bright, is he? And he does not seem to be able to speak very well." He laughed.

It was now Hedgehog's turn to splutter a noise. "Not very bright…Oh look here's you. Yes, Murdoch is *so* you!" They both watched the screen as a rather mad man talked to a sock on his hand.

"The man is an idiot! A fool!"

Hedgehog smiled, "Well…"

"Yes, thank you," snapped Pink Rabbit. "Now here, 'Face' – he is attractive, dashing."

"Too late, you already chose Murdoch."

"Ssh, you two, this is the bit where the 'plan comes together' – I love these bits." They sat back and watched a series of contraptions and traps which foiled the baddies brilliantly.

"Cool," said Hedgehog.

"Yes, the show does have a certain attraction. 'Cool' could be befitting." Pink Rabbit took a final sip of his cocktail.

"Now <u>that's</u> how to bring a plan together!" declared EG.

Chapter 12

Another Unnecessary Saving

"I reckon it should be dark enough now," said EG. Pink Rabbit and Hedgehog had both chosen to snooze whilst waiting for night to fall. EG had used the time to make the 'improvement' to her mini fridge. Not having a coloured bulb, she'd painted the inside of the light cover so that the existing bulb now shone through a deep, rich purple – a Professor Plum purple. (She had a huge stash of paints, particularly tester pots, which people were always looking to get rid of – perfect for just when she 'needed' them). So now, as she opened the door, a purple haze covered the Fabs, reflecting off the silvery walls, making the ice-lollies look like precious jewels. (Which she already knew they were!)

Her two friends woke up slowly: Pink Rabbit gently lifted an ear from one eye and, as he blinked his way out of his slumber and his eyes began to focus, he seemed almost surprised at the world around him. Hedgehog stretched his short arms above his head, his waistcoat stretched to its limit over his round tummy and gave a satisfied sigh. The faint glimmer of light from the few tea-light candles, that EG had lit earlier, were flickering to an end. The darkness beyond their hideout hung heavy and intense. EG was not scared of the dark, but on looking out, felt that the darkness looked so thick that it seemed solid. Above them, the Three Trees stood brooding and somehow alert to any incoming danger which might threaten the three P.O.N.D. detectives. Grabbing their torches, all three then gathered everything up. The wood was piled in a wheelbarrow, with everything else balanced hopefully on top. Leaving the last flame to ebb away alone, EG heaved up the handles of the wheelbarrow, with the other two each holding on to a side. Having agreed earlier that they were clearly not going to be able to exit through their normal route - over a muddy beck and holding on to tree roots - they made their way through the wooded copse which protected P.O.N.D. from sight of the village. From the back of the thicket of trees, they had to cross Sutton's paddock which held a few sheep and pigs. EG had to quickly stop Pink Rabbit from squealing when he nearly bumped into a sheep that was grazing quietly.

"What was that ferocious woolly thing?!" Then, when he stepped on what he described as small squelchy things, exclaimed: "What do you mean poo? Sheep's poo? Why do they do them so small and black? How is one supposed to see them in the dark?"

"What, are yours pink and luminous?" smirked Hedgehog.

"I shall choose to ignore that question."

"Mind the pigs," said EG "They're always getting out their pens and coming over into our garden. And Dad seems to think it's my job to go get Mrs

Sutton and then help get them back. Though it's quite fun actually. But I don't tell Dad that."

"Do they attack?" asked Pink Rabbit nervously.

They bounced the wheelbarrow carefully across the paddock. They then had to creep down the garden path of the Sutton's back garden, which led down the side of the house and out to the front, and in turn on to the village high street. EG glanced at her house, which was opposite the Sutton's – a few lights were on. Pink Rabbit watched her but said nothing. Up through the village, past Creepy Tree. (Named by EG, because one of the few streetlights stood right behind it, forming unnerving shadows through the sprawling oak branches. Both the shadows and branches felt like they would nip at your heels as you walked past.) Pink Rabbit shuddered and stole a hurried glance over his shoulder.

Once past the village shop, they came to the crossroads at the top of the village, left was down to Ingleby Cross, right to East Harlsey and straight over was the water tower. They were just about to cross when EG spotted something 'useful' at the bottom of a hedge.

"Not now EG," hissed Hedgehog and Pink Rabbit in unison. She paused momentarily, a little torn, but then carried on pushing the wheelbarrow. Arms aching, she lowered the handles down in front of the water tower. It was like a square, mini Tudor turret, made from huge chunks of time-worn stone.

"The door's round the back," said EG, lifting the handles once more. Inside the heavy, wooden door was a metal staircase leading up to a platform. The platform overlooked a huge, metal, open tank, filled with water. It took them three trips up and down the stairs to haul everything into position.

Once finished, Pink Rabbit peered over the metal railings into the tank. There was one single narrow window at the back of the tower, sitting alone like a slot for archers in a castle. It let in a sliver of pearly moonlight. "Oh my carrot tops! This water is extremely black – are you sure it is water and not ink?"

"The piranhas are going to work really well in there. Brilliant, EG." added Hedgehog.

"Indeed. I am beginning to think this is rather a good plan."

She smiled broadly. It felt nice being complimented by Pink Rabbit. "Yeah. And it's freezing in there."

Pink Rabbit shivered and pulled a face. "Oh, how freezing?" He leant over the railings to dip in his hand, edged a bit further to almost reach. Then suddenly a reach too far, and splash! He was in! Swallowed up by the darkness.

Spluttering to the surface, he gulped in both air and water. "Can't – glug – swim! – glug – my fur! – glug - my pinkdom!"

"You don't need to panic!" shouted EG. "Kick your legs! Reach for my hand!"

Next to her, Hedgehog was already climbing the railings, having whipped off his waistcoat and with majestic ease, he dived into the icy blackness and surfaced precisely in front of Pink Rabbit. He shouted at him to relax, then gripped the rabbit under his chin from behind, in text-book life-saving style, and swam backwards pulling Pink Rabbit with him.

"Get your ears out of my face!"

Immediately the rabbit's ears collapsed limply to either side of his head. At the platform Hedgehog used his shoulder, then hands, to push Pink Rabbit up while EG hauled by his arm. Pink Rabbit flopped onto his back on the ice-cold metal, his chest heaving. Beside him, Hedgehog also laid flat out, every breath thick and heavy.

"You saved my life," gasped Pink Rabbit.

Both Hedgehog and Pink Rabbit tilted their heads to look sideways at each other, water dripping from their faces. "Yeah, but don't tell all the pink rabbits or they'll all want saving!" answered Hedgehog, through deep breaths. Pink Rabbit chuckled.

EG finally spoke. "But you weren't actually in any danger, you know. I did try and tell you. It's only about chest height on the side where you were – there's a ledge round the edge. It's the middle that's deep. Look." And she put a piece of the wood in and pulled it out. The water mark barely reached halfway up.

Hedgehog and Pink Rabbit both looked at each other again, then at EG, then back to each other.

Abruptly, Pink Rabbit sat up on his elbows. "So, technically, *technically,* you did not actually save me. You were being all rather unnecessary. Jolly good. Excellent." With that, he stood up and, with finesse, shook out his fur so that it was almost dry and silky again.

Hedgehog spluttered, trying to get his round body up. "But you didn't know that! You were the Panic King! You were the one being all 'unnecessary' – you'd probably drown in a puddle the way you and your pinkdom flail around!"

"I was just a little shocked by the chill of the water and then I was merely considering which stroke to employ to swim back to the side."

"Pink Rabbit you were a bit…er…mad," agreed EG. She turned to Hedgehog. "You were amazing – I didn't know you could even swim, let alone like that."

Hedgehog puffed out his chest. "Woodland Diving Champion, three years running in my youth. There's always a 'Free Diving and High Diving Inter-Woodland Competition' at Cod Beck Reservoir at Osmotherley village. Good to see it's all still there." He added, flexing his arms into a diving position once more.

Pink Rabbit muttered under his breath, "Totally unnecessary."

"Come on you two, let's get out of here. With all that noise someone's probably heard us. But maybe they'll just think we're ghosts or something," said EG.

"Or one weird pink ghost, more like." said Hedgehog.

They all made their way down the stairwell, Hedgehog's small feet squelching a little with each step.

****

EG opened the backdoor very quietly, she knew Mum wouldn't be back from London yet – when she saw clients down there, she always returned really late. She said she found it a drag, but EG couldn't see why she did it then. Stepping slowly in, she wasn't sure if her dad would still be up. Once upstairs, she saw a light escaping from the bottom of the door to his study. He grandly called it a 'study' but it was just the spare room converted into a home office. However, her sister's bedroom door was open, and the room empty. So, Lulu wasn't in – staying at her friend's house as usual. She was hardly ever here these days. Clearly no-one had missed her. Her Mum always assumed Dad was on top of things when she wasn't there. Wrong! EG really missed how life was before, when she felt she had a family who even noticed that she wasn't in the house. Hedgehog and Pink Rabbit felt more like family now. Even Pink Rabbit, who'd only been around for a few weeks, she realised with surprise, felt like someone she'd known for years.

She smiled at the memories of the day. It had been funny when Pink Rabbit had fallen in and had gone into extreme panic. And then both their faces when they'd found out that there'd been no danger after all. She didn't mind their bickering – sometimes it was annoying, but mostly it felt, well, homely. The sort of things families do.

The question was, could she keep them under control long enough to pull off this grand plan?

Chapter 13

Revealing the Truth

EG heaved open the water tower door, then immediately let it swing to. Something yellow and grubby was nestling in the overgrown grass. Smiling, she picked up a tatty old tennis ball and shoved it in her jacket pocket. Heaving the door once more, she bounded up the metal stairs two at a time and found Pink Rabbit peering curiously into the black water. She tossed the ball into the equipment box by his feet. Watching it fall, he rolled his eyes, "I cannot see of what use that disgusting tennis ball will ever be."

EG shrugged. "No, I can't now, but one day I will. Usually everything's got a use."

Her friend looked straight at her. "Yes, everything has its purpose in this world. And it is down to us to discover our own true purpose – no-one else will."

EG looked back at him, confused. She felt somewhere in her that he was making sense, but her brain said he wasn't. "That's a bit…er…deep."

"Much like this water – in the centre of course," he smiled. "Its appearance has not improved at all in the daylight. I think I was right to be concerned as I swam out of it last night."

"Swam? You looked like you were having a fit." she teased gently.

Pink Rabbit chose to ignore this. "Ah, here is our little friend."

Hedgehog gasped for breath as he reached the top step. He stood for a moment clutching the banister, drawing in air.

"A little unfit, are we?"

"No! I ran all the way, cos I was late."

"Yes, and it is no doubt harder for you as you are a little," he searched for the right word. "Stumpy."

"Not stumpy!" He straightened up, his breath settling. "Just hedgehog sized."

"Anyway you two, let's get things set up. I thought we'd tie the planks to the railings, round the top with those old skipping ropes – thought it'd be quieter than hammering them in somewhere."

Hedgehog's small hands weaved the ends of rope over and under, in and out, secure knot after secure knot. Meanwhile, Pink Rabbit fumbled, at one point somehow tying his own leg to a plank. "Not a good knots-man then? Never been a sailor? Not met Christopher Columbus or Blackbeard?" asked Hedgehog sarcastically.

"It is just a little harder than it looks."

"Oh, give it here." He lifted the heavy rope and deftly set to work. After a while he stood up and stretched his back, his brow glistening slightly from the effort. Mid-way through his stretch he saw Pink

Rabbit leaning against the wall, very relaxed. "I've done all the work!" Hedgehog said indignantly.

"I gave the moral support that you needed. I shall see if EG requires some similar assistance."

Already EG had fitted a small battery-operated pump to a long plastic tube. Using a long pole, Pink Rabbit helped loop the tube around some existing metal hooks in the ceiling and stone walls. Once it was secure, EG gave it a test run. Pink Rabbit stood well back as the pump gulped up water from the tank and squirted it powerfully through the tubing. Water then erupted from the tube through EG's carefully calculated holes, attacking the room like a series of police water cannons. EG watched for a few moments analysing the effect. Satisfied with the result, she flicked the off switch and covered the pump so that it was out of sight. They then all set to work putting everything else in place. After quite a lot of hard lifting and moving and readjusting, EG stood back with her hands on her hips.

"Do you think it's enough?"

"I think it's brilliant!" said Hedgehog, with an excited gleam in his eye.

"Most certainly a plan that will come together," added Pink Rabbit.

****

EG heard Pink Rabbit and Hedgehog before she saw them.

"Stop pushing!"

"I am unable to see in this squatted position!"

"Then move your great fluffiness over a bit then!"

"As you are well aware, there is a large mound of mud there, which will play havoc with the tuft of my tail."

"Ssh, you two. Everyone'll realise you're there."

Her two friends were hidden behind a hedge in the Sedgewick's front garden – she knew the family were on holiday, so Pink Rabbit and Hedgehog were supposedly out of sight. She heard them settle down, so she gingerly made her way up the high street. She felt a bit stupid and hoped no-one would recognise her as she was now in disguise. Then she told herself 'confidence', and stood a little taller and walked with more purpose, which was difficult in high heels and a tight skirt.

She'd managed to get out of the house without anyone seeing her – which wasn't hard as Mum still wasn't back yet and Lulu was already, or still, out, and Dad already, or still, in his study, working from home. He *never* noticed anything, and just to prove it she had gone round the front door and knocked - in full disguise. 'Let's see if he recognises his own daughter,' she'd thought. EG had pretended to be collecting for charity; he'd simply rummaged in his pocket and handed over some change, never once noticing who she was.

As she walked up the high street now, she ruefully made a mental note to put the money in the charity box in the village shop next time she was in. She checked her black wig was straight – she'd used a cool iron to make it all flat and smooth and was pleased with the glossy look. Using a mixture of her sister's make-up and some special effects make-up (she was always ordering 'useful' things online) she'd been able to make herself look a lot older, and, if she said so herself, glamorous. The fake, aging lines round her eyes and mouth looked real. She blinked a few times: she wasn't sure how women wore such long, false eyelashes – she just hoped they wouldn't get stuck together.

It didn't take her long to spot the gang of bullies hanging around outside the village school. EG made as if to walk past them then turned and put on, what she hoped, was a look of surprise and being incredibly impressed. When the girls saw her, they nudged each other and glowered. EG walked confidently over to them – she was now definitely 'in role'.

"Please don't frown," she said. "You'll ruin the whole look." She held up her fingers as if she was making a picture frame around the girls. They all looked at each other, unsure what to make of this woman in front of them. "You're just what I'm looking for!" exclaimed EG, getting out her professional looking camera and snapping a couple of pictures.

Despite themselves, the girls couldn't help standing ready for the next shot.

"Who are you anyway?" asked Pug Face, squinting, which only made her eyes sink even deeper into her face.

With a swish of her over-styled brown hair, Big One gave Pug Face a sharp elbow in the ribs, as if to say, 'I'm the leader of this gang and I do the talking'. Looking suitably told off, Pug Face stepped back.

EG handed over a business card that she'd made: 'Senior Photographer and Model Scout, Cosmopolitan Magazine'. Big One read it out, her eyes shining with excitement through her thick, clumpy mascara.

Curious, Pug Face peered over Big One's shoulder and said, "Really?" in a sarcastic tone. Her friend shoved her and hissed that she shut up.

"I go to unusual places to find new faces to be models in our magazine. Not everyone can get down to London can they? I've been going round a few towns and villages in North Yorkshire, as we're looking for a group of trendsetters. I did find some girls yesterday, who were really keen, but now that I've found you, I think you'll be much better. Obviously if you'd rather not, I'll go back to them…" EG wasn't sure if her 'grown-up' voice sounded real enough, so casually flicked through the photos on her camera, as if looking back at the other girls.

Immediately, the gang preened themselves and insisted that they were very keen. "What do we have to do?"

"Well, you've got this retro-modern look that's so individual and very clever." The girls grinned eagerly. "With a nautical twist." The girls looked blank. "A bit sailory – piratey." She explained quickly. The girls looked down at themselves, unsure. "All very South of France chic!" EG added even more quickly. This brought smug looks. "What we need is a beautiful background with water in maybe, that'll really enhance your look. Is there a river or anything round here?"

The group looked a bit vague. "Well, there's a beck down Ingleby Cross – the village down the hill," Ginger One offered unenthusiastically, her long orange hair hanging limply down her back.

Pug Face pulled a face that made her look even uglier. "Yeah, but it's all muddy down there in't it? We'll ruin our shoes."

Everyone nodded in agreement.

"Well, I did happen to see a beautiful old water tower as I came into the village. The stonework would add a lovely contrast to your ultra-modern look."

Seeing their dubious expressions and worried that she was losing them, EG found herself getting more over-dramatic.

"It'll be amazing with light streaming in behind you. It'll be atmospheric – so cool! And I'm sure once my editor sees the photos, she'll be dying to get you booked for future work too. It pays well…."

At the mention of money, there were mutterings of approval; it was almost as if pound signs had kerchinged into their eyes.

Behind the hedge, Pink Rabbit whispered into Hedgehog's ear, "I think they are falling for it!"

"Ssh," said Hedgehog with a scowl, flipping a long rabbit ear out of his face.

Ginger One looked down the road, momentarily puzzled, then shook her head and looked away. Hedgehog and Pink Rabbit ducked down even further, bumping their heads as they did so.

"I've got to go soon, so can we do this now?" EG asked, looking at her watch. The bullies now couldn't agree fast enough. As they walked to the water tower, the girls kept pulling out various bits of make-up and touching up their already heavily made-up faces.

Suddenly, EG's eyes widened. A prickle of sweat crawled down her back. Her sister Lulu was walking down the street towards her, chatting and laughing with a friend. EG held her head firmly up, eyes glued forward on the horizon, whilst trying not to trip in her heels. 'Don't look at me!' thought EG. 'Don't look at me!' As Lulu came level with them, she glanced at EG vaguely then walked past. EG let out a tiny sigh. Then after a moment, Lulu paused, looked over her shoulder and frowned. Feeling her sister's eyes boring into the back of her head, EG tried to keep walking normally. She felt heat rising up her cheeks. Finally, Lulu shrugged and carried on walking, chatting to her friend. EG quickly pulled herself together, realising she'd been holding her breath.

In the meantime, Pink Rabbit and Hedgehog were almost left behind as they were too busy squabbling about whose head hit whose. They scampered to catch up, then dived over another hedge to keep out of Lulu's sight.

Once at the tower, Pug Face stared at the building, shuddered and said, "It's a bit creepy in't it?" It took EG a moment to answer because she was struck by how pathetic this Oompa Loompa orange girl, with her fashion victim clothes, looked against the beauty of the listed building. She almost felt sorry for her. Almost.

Remembering Joey, she said, "No, no, atmospheric! The sort of thing in the best music videos. I've got some candles in my bag, I'll light them once we're inside – that'll add to the photos and look great in the magazine!" EG ushered them all in quickly, before they changed their minds. Hesitantly, the girls teetered their way up, their heels clanging on the metal stairs. Once upstairs, EG swiftly lit the candles that she had already placed strategically around the room, so that their shadows hid some of the equipment.

"What are those planks for?" asked Big One, suspiciously.

"Oh, I don't know. Probably left by workmen checking for something or other. But, actually they'd be great! You could be like gorgeous pirates walking the plank – now that would really add the finishing touch. If you all posed on one – because look, there's enough for one each. But let me get a few photos standing here." She immediately started snapping away on her camera.

Like amoeba reacting to light, the girls responded instantly, showing off for the camera in what they thought were model-like poses, but which EG just thought looked grotesque.

"Brilliant! Stunning! Beautiful!" she shouted at them all.

Meanwhile, Pink Rabbit and Hedgehog attempted to sneak up the stairs very quietly. Pink Rabbit had put his hands on Hedgehog's back to push him up, causing Hedgehog to slap his hands away. EG heard the skirmish and spoke a bit louder.

"Now if you stand on the planks, I can get the light shining through the window behind you. Like a heavenly light. This could even make the front cover of the magazine! And probably go viral on social media!"

She then suggested they take off their shoes, that maybe barefoot would make it look more like an exotic beach. "It'll be like a celebrity Instagram story!" EG added enthusiastically They all took off their shoes and tossed them onto the platform –except Big One.

"What's wrong?" asked Squatty, looking even more square without the height of her high heels. "We'll look good barefoot."

"It's just…I don't want to alright!" Big One snapped back.

Pug Face frowned, wondering why her friend didn't want to take off her shoes.

At EG's encouragement, the girls edged a little further along their planks.

Pink Rabbit and Hedgehog were now hidden in the shadows on the platform. "I shall go round to the other side and get ready to wind up the 'piranhas'," whispered Pink Rabbit.

Hedgehog was confused. This wasn't what they'd all agreed.

"It will allow me more time. You remain poised to operate the water pump." Pink Rabbit slipped away before Hedgehog could argue. He then heard EG shout pointedly,

"We need a bit more atmosphere!" This was the agreed cue to start the water pump. Hedgehog quickly flicked the switch and water immediately shot out from every single hole in the tube, surrounding the bullies like an army of rapid-fire water guns. Barely able to see, and gasping for breath, the girls screamed and started to stumble. There was just enough time to squeeze out a few swear words (some EG had never even heard of before) before they all flopped heavily into the middle of the water tank, creating huge splashes that licked right up the sides of the tower walls.

Ginger One managed to surface first. With the half ton of hair products now washed out, her hair actually shone a rich red as it clung to her face. "Help us! My watch!" She tried to tread water, holding up one arm, in an attempt to save her watch.

As the others splashed to the surface, like deformed mammals emerging for the first time from the depths of the sea, they screeched and wailed,

"It's freezing! Oh my God!"

"My make-up's running!"

"What about my hair extensions?!"

Legs kicking out haphazardly, they tried to tread water. But kept sinking, as they insisted on tipping back their heads in a vain attempt to keep the water from going any further on to their faces, and make-up.

EG shouted above the splashing and moaning. "You've got away with bullying people for too long! Making people do things they don't want to. Well, not anymore. Look at you now. Look at who you really are! Look at your streaky fake tan, your weird eyes with false eyelashes hanging off and mascara drooling down your cheeks. And, oh dear, some of you now have green hair – your over bleached hair must have reacted with the chlorine in the water."

The girls looked at each other aghast, screamed and threw their hands to their faces, still barely able to stay above the water.

171

"Look at you, you always made out you had 'naturally olive skin'!" said Pug Face to Big One, wiping a finger down Big One's face, creating another streak in the fake tan. "But really, you're so white you're almost blue!"

Ginger One looked at Squatty, "I <u>knew</u> those were hair extensions. And you had the nerve to always make sarky comments about *my* hair!" she snapped angrily, still trying to keep her watch out of the water.

Big One glared at EG and made an attempt to get to the edge. "So what! We'll just put our make-up back on as soon as we get out – no-one else'll know! Who are you really, anyway?"

Clicking away at her camera, EG said, "Yes, they will. If I put these photos up on the school's Instagram."

"You can't do that, only teachers have access," snarled Squatty, her extensions almost completely out, her hair now looking really thin and masculine.

"Oh it's easy to get past their security, if you know what you're doing."

Big One made to argue again, but then said, "Oh shut up! I'm getting out of here." And started to doggy-paddle with her head tilted back.

"Not till you promise never to bully anyone <u>ever</u> again."

"Yes. Whatever." said Ginger One instantly. "Don't know why I did this 'shoot' anyway. I've just got to go."

"You're joking," said Pug Face. "You gave in quick enough! No way, I say!" The others all pouted in agreement and then swam to the side, jabbing at the water like five-year-olds, sinking slightly with every stroke from the weight of their wet clothes.

EG then bent down and picked up a plastic box with water in; she saw Pink Rabbit's hands quickly drop in a pile of small objects. She then tipped the contents of the box into the water – everything plopped in.

Pug Face screamed. "What was that you poured in?"

The objects quickly started to whizz around the bullies, both round their legs and just beneath the surface. The black water was too dark and ominous to see exactly what they were.

"You're not scared of a few piranha fish, are you? Mind your bare toes though, they'll be easy to chew off!"

Panicked screams reverberated round the small tower, echoing off the cold walls.

"Don't be stupid, they can't be real piranhas," said Ginger One. "I'm getting out."

"Ah! I felt one."

"So did I! They're all over me!"

"Ow! Make them stop!"

EG took more photos. "So, do you promise?"

"Yes," They all shrieked, spinning round and round and hitting randomly at the water.

"You promise to never bully anyone ever again?"

"Yes!!" they all screamed again, even louder.

"Good. Remember, I'll always have these pictures." As she spoke, she used the long pole to unhook the tubing round the room. Surreptitiously, Hedgehog wrapped up the pump and Pink Rabbit gathered up the candles; they both then quietly made their way downstairs with the equipment. As EG walked to the top of the stairs, Big One shouted, "But what about us? What about these, these…? Ah! Another one! How do we get out of here?" With each question her voice became more and more hysterical.

"Oh, they calm down after a while."

She was almost at the bottom step when she could just make out Squatty saying a little nervously, "I don't think I feel them anymore."

All the bullies heaved themselves out of the water, some looking like beached whales. Big One's shoes slipped off as she clambered out and dragged herself to her feet, hampered by her sodden clothes.

Slack-jawed the girls stared at their 'leader'.

Pug Face was the first to speak. "Oh my God, you're tiny!" She looked up, and down again, then bent down to pick up a high heeled shoe that was bobbing in the water. Big One made to grab it off her. "Look at your shoe!" Scornfully pulling the shoe open, she showed it to the rest. "Look she's got built up insoles – fake insides to make her look taller." Pug Face turned her snub face back to Big One, who was stock still, unsure what to do. "You're pathetic!" she shouted, jabbing an angry finger at her. "You were always bragging about how you were so lovely and tall, taller than the rest of us. You're the most fake of us all! We can't trust anything you say again. Come on everyone, let's leave this *tiny* loser!"

Hiding downstairs, EG, Pink Rabbit and Hedgehog tried to stifle their sniggers. They silently hi-fived each other, then crouched low again as the bullies sploshed down the stairs and away.

Once they were gone, the three dashed upstairs to collect the remains of the plan. With a fishing net in each hand, EG scooped out all the 'piranhas'.

"All those years of collecting wind-up, plastic toys finally paid off, ay EG?" said Hedgehog, smiling, looking at the submarine, frog, mermaid and many others of all shapes and sizes.

"Yeah, I knew they'd be useful one day!" Once they'd finished, they stood up, looking proud of themselves. "Now this definitely deserves a celebration Fab – Joey is finally free!" Pink Rabbit and Hedgehog both laughed. "Yes, he won't have to worry about being bullied again, that's for sure!" agreed Hedgehog with a grin.

Chapter 14

Client Confidentiality

Back at P.O.N.D., EG lined up the wind-up toys on the windowsill of the shed and smiled. Once her glorious new Fab mirror had been set up, she opened her fridge – a beautiful, amethyst purple glow shone from inside. Noting that she only had two Fabs left, she told herself off for not being vigilant. She then came back out to her denim deckchair to find Hedgehog already sucking a chocolate lime and settled very comfortably in his wicker seat. As he shuffled down even further, he shook his paper bag and he too noted that he was getting low on his required sweets.

Just about to check her tongue in the mirror, EG was distracted by Pink Rabbit as he prepared the most extravagant cocktail. She couldn't quite see what all the ingredients were, but it seemed to be a pinch of one thing then a spoon of another, then a dash of something else – he was so quick. He then took up his silver cocktail shaker and shook it exuberantly over each shoulder, accompanied by a small wiggle-bottom dance. Despairing of the rabbit, Hedgehog shook his head and rolled his boiled sweet round his mouth. The drink finally complete, Pink Rabbit poured the solution over a strainer, not into his usual wide cocktail glass, but into a highball tumbler. Holding it up to the light, he nodded his head in quiet triumph: the drink gently paled from dark orange at the bottom to light orange at the top. With a small flourish of his hand, he popped in a paper pineapple on a stick and then he too settled down in his hammock and began to sip, making rather satisfied noises.

EG smiled, feeling a contentment she always did sitting with her friends. She screwed up her ice-lolly wrapper then looked at it pensively. "You know," she said out loud, but actually more to herself. "I could use this to …Yeah, I'm sure I could. Don't know why I'm not already doing it!"

"'Ooin' wha'?" asked Hedgehog, looking up from his paper bag, his mouth full of chocolate lime.

"Creating my own energy."

"Yes," said Pink Rabbit with his velvet ears over his eyes, glass in hand. "It is always good to create one's own energy."

"My generator is always packing up – it's no wonder Dad wanted to throw it out. And I hate it when I lose power-"

"As do I," interjected Pink Rabbit.

"-as the computer obviously goes down."

Hedgehog asked, "Ow d'yer 'oo 'at?"

"I thought that we were celebrating. Relax a little EG," said Pink Rabbit, ears still over his eyes.

She opened her mouth to answer Hedgehog, then stopped. "You're right, we are celebrating."

Hedgehog looked shocked. He knew how hard it was for EG not to immediately start work on an idea as soon as it came into her head. Was the rabbit having a good influence on her? He shook his head as if to get the thought out.

All three slipped into retelling the highlights of the day, laughing and congratulating themselves.

"Tell me though, Little Spiky One. In which part of it were you Mr T? In which part were you fearsomely strong?"

"All the way through my pink friend, all the way through!"

They all laughed.

At the end Hedgehog asked, "What now? No more mysteries for the time being."

"I'm going to work on my generator plan – I think it'll be really cool. And I'm still working on our Pledge of Allegiance."

"Come to think of it, I should spend a bit of time at home now – we've been out so much."

"We do have to let our 'client' know that we have solved his case. Mr Cuttlewell will be very pleased with us, I am sure," said Pink Rabbit.

"Of course. Well done, Pink Rabbit," said Hedgehog, before he could stop himself.

"Why, I thank you Mr Hedgehog. And so it is, that I do have some good ideas after all." Pink Rabbit smiled wryly at him.

"Well, I wouldn't go that far," mumbled Hedgehog.

"Yes, we should go up to the shop. It's all part of the service," agreed EG.

"And we can collect my finest carrots."

"Oh yes, Mr Cuttlewell said we'd all get something if we caught the thief," said Hedgehog. He then turned to EG. "But perhaps you'll need to go back to being EG first."

"Uh?" She grabbed her mirror for a proper look at herself. She'd been so busy watching Pink Rabbit make his cocktail that she'd not looked in the mirror and not realised that she still had on her disguise. As she pulled off her sleek wig and huge false eyelashes and wiped off the make-up, she thought about how much she'd enjoyed being in disguise. It had felt quite liberating to be someone else, not 'EG'. Reading the etched words on her mirror *Truly See Yourself. See yourself As The World Sees You.*, she thought perhaps the opposite was true. To not be the person other people always saw, or *thought* they saw, that could be freeing. She hoped she'd get the opportunity to be in disguise again.

"We should ask Mr Cuttlewell if we can put up a poster in his shop, advertising. P.O.N.D. services," she said.

"Good idea," agreed Hedgehog. "Let's ask old 'Grumpy-Drawers'."

"Do you mind?" said Pink Rabbit, indignantly.

Hedgehog smirked." I wasn't referring to you – it's Mr Cuttlewell, he's always grumpy. But if you see yourself as a Grumpy-Drawers. Well, yes." He peered at him as if he was wearing a pair of Victorian drawers, remembering how Pink Rabbit had teased him looking for his tail.

"Look all you want my friend. But be warned, you may well end up with pinkness envy."

Hedgehog turned away hurriedly. "Poohf".

As they left, Pink Rabbit picked up EG's Fab bag, "He did say a box of Fabs for you!"

*****

The bell on the shop door pinged as the three friends walked in. Pink Rabbit glanced up at the bell - EG quickly ushered him in.

Mrs Cuttlewell looked up from her pricing gun. She was clearly not best pleased to see them because she immediately looked back down at the tins of peaches in front her and carried on pricing up. At the sound of the bell, Mr Cuttlewell hurried in from the back room with a smile fixed on his face, which instantly fell when he saw who the 'customers' were.

"What d' you three want?"

"We've solved the case!" said EG proudly. And she went on to explain the reason why things had been going missing from the shop, that bullies had forced someone to do it, but that they had now sorted it all out and the shop would be safe from now on!

Mrs Cuttlewell made an odd kind of noise, but one that clearly said she doubted it.

Her husband looked thoughtfully at them. "Well, 'appen, nowt's bin tekun int last couple a days. I'll give thee that." He stroked his chin, contemplating the information.

"Can I just remind you, dear Sir, of our agreement? That, on solving the case, we, all three, be entitled to some kind of reward," Pink Rabbit hopped forward, looking round the shop for carrots.

"Uh, did ah now?"

"Well, 'oo did it then?" interrupted Mrs Cuttlewell, putting down her pricing gun.

Pink Rabbit and Hedgehog both opened their mouths to answer, but EG quickly spoke over them.

"We can't say."

"What?! It's ower shop, we've a right t' know, young lass. And 'appen the police'll think the same an' all." Both husband and wife continued to press EG for the information, but she stood firm.

"The person who did it, didn't want to do it at all. They were forced into it, so I don't think they should be punished."

"What abou' these bullies, then, what are their names?" asked Mrs Cuttlewell.

"Pug Face, Squatty, Big One-" began Pink Rabbit.

Getting extremely exasperated, Mrs Cuttlewell snapped, "Them's not names! I'm callin' the police right now!" And she started to pull out her phone.

EG's face took on a strength and determination that even Hedgehog had not seen before.

"It's about stopping the crime, isn't it? Solving the mystery. Not about punishing someone who has been punished enough. More than enough. Do you really want this poor person dragged off to a police station to make their life even more miserable, is that what you want to do?"

Mrs Cuttlewell turned round to face EG. She was secretly impressed by the girl, but wasn't going to say it, so instead said,

"Humpf! We're out of pocket yer know, all this thievin'".

"Ah, that reminds me," said EG, and pulled out a handful of change from her pocket and put it in the charity box on the counter. "My dad wanted to give to charity," she added simply.

"I suppose it's good it's all stopped. So, er… well done," said Mr Cuttlewell, begrudgingly.

All this time Pink Rabbit had been peering round the shop looking for carrots: lifting lids of boxes, pressing his nose against the glass of the deli counter, opening the small freezer. As he lifted the freezer lid, he knocked the pricing gun with his elbow and managed to set it on automatic, so that it now fired off price stickers at random all over Mrs Cuttlewell. She snatched up the gun, growled at Pink Rabbit and marched off into the back room, with her forehead marked at £1.16.

"Our reward then, Mr Cuttlewell?" queried Pink Rabbit, oblivious to the shopkeeper's glower.

"Moondust again, Pink'un?"

"No thank you!" said Pink Rabbit firmly. "That is a most dangerous substance. Enormous fun, but dangerous nonetheless."

The shopkeeper couldn't help smiling. He handed each of them their 'reward': a box of Fabs, a huge bag of chocolate limes and a bunch of bright orange carrots, still with their leafy, green tops.

When EG mentioned the possibility of putting up a poster in the shop to advertise their detective services, he looked bemused.

"So, yer think yer all Sherlock 'olmes do yer? Aye, ah'll put up a poster and ah might even recommend yer! It'll be interestin t' see what yer get up t'. E's part of it too is 'ee?" He nodded in the direction of Pink Rabbit.

"Oh yes," said EG.

"Aye, this should *very* intrestin'."

They left happily with their rewards, Pink Rabbit having already started crunching into a carrot. As they meandered down the village high street they spotted Joey, familiar in his assortment of clothes, some too big, some too small. EG shouted to him, wanting to tell him the good news that the bullies wouldn't be hassling him anymore. But Joey only half looked round and carried on. As EG shouted again, he actually seemed to speed up.

She was really puzzled. "Why is he ignoring us?"

"Maybe he just had to get home." Hedgehog shrugged.

"But I thought he lived over the fields past Big Arm Tree."

Hedgehog shrugged again. "Speaking of home, I best get back."

EG and Pink Rabbit watched as Hedgehog also sped up and dashed off home.

"He really does need a proper tail," said Pink Rabbit, between bites of his carrot.

EG looked at him and shook her head.

As they came to EG's house, there were a couple of lights showing in the falling dusk.

"Is your mother home now?" asked Pink Rabbit.

"Yes, she…I don't know." Then she frowned, looking at her friend. "I didn't know I'd said that she was away."

"Yes, the other day," answered said Pink Rabbit vaguely. "Anyway, you are always a little…different when she is away."

"Am I?!"

Pink Rabbit moved to walk her to her door.

"I'd better go in, Mum'll have tea ready. I'll see you tomorrow," she said hurriedly.

Pink Rabbit smiled and stepped back. "Of course. I am sure I will meet your mother *one day*. I shall have to." And with that he bounced off.

EG stood looking after him. 'Have to'? Why 'have to'? She said to herself. Pink Rabbit seemed to gradually disappear into the failing light. She glanced up at the lights in her house then back to her friend, but he was now gone. So she turned and, without realising it, hunched up her shoulders and walked into the house.

Chapter 15

Waste Not, Want Not

EG didn't see Hedgehog for days. She wasn't sure how many as the days seemed to blur into each other while she beavered away on her idea for a generator. With sketches and half-made mini models everywhere, she felt she was getting closer each day to a final working machine.

Pink Rabbit either watched or listened from his hammock, using the time to catch up on some snoozes. It amused him to see her arrive each morning with some new bit of rubbish that she'd found. But without fail he'd then see it attached or used in the generator.

As the days wore on, he started to hear chugs or whirs, then silence. A cog or screw or strip of rubber would be tossed aside, then more chugs as the small monster was attempted to be brought to life. Pink Rabbit knew well enough to stay away. EG was so engrossed that she mostly forgot that he was there, only really noticing when he snored. It was an odd snore – it almost had an electrical crackle to it. But maybe her mind was in over-drive, as she was all things electrical at the moment. Anyway, she found it oddly comforting. Unlike her dad's snores, which were almost unworldly: deep, resonant rumbles that made you think the whole room was vibrating, or maybe that he was trying to communicate with whales 500 miles away. Mum and Lulu were always on at him to lose weight to stop the snoring. 'Oh, yes.' He'd say dismissively.

She was brought back from her thoughts by a sudden, smooth thrum – the generator was finally working. "Yes," she shouted, both arms raised in triumph.

Casually lifting an ear from one eye, Pink Rabbit said flatly, "Well done." And gently lowered the ear. Then added from his darkness, "What is it then, this fine machine of yours?"

"It's a Garbo-Generator. That's what I'm calling it anyway. It generates electricity only using garbage - waste items."

She filled a funnel at the top with wrappers and other rubbish she'd hoarded and stepped back to watch as it came to life. The generator chugged gently, slowly releasing chemicals from the rubbish. Attached to the machine were small containers that collected the by-product chemicals, such as nitrogen, that EG knew were bound to be useful for something else!

"Hmm, and what would normally happen to waste, if not used?"

EG wasn't sure if he was being sarcastic or not. She was also a bit disappointed at his underwhelming response. It was normally her parents that couldn't be bothered to be interested in her life. With a small twist of her mouth, she set to work fixing leads and wires from the generator to various electrical points in the shed.

Noticing her disappointment, Pink Rabbit added more enthusiastically, "Quite ingenious! You do like to make sure everything in this world is as it should be – waste used, people protected. And it is surprisingly quiet, this machine of yours. I did think it might be heard by passers-by. But no."

"Yeah, I worked on sound-proofing it. But I think we might need some security here generally, maybe a bit of camouflage. I've got a few ideas I've been working on-"

"Of course."

"- cos we do need to know if anyone's coming."

At that moment Hedgehog and Fenella arrived, making EG jump. Fenella was wearing a hat that EG had not seen before, a hot pink one, like a short top hat. Pink Rabbit immediately jumped off his hammock and bounced up to greet Fenella, kissing her gallantly on the hand and asking if she was well.

Hedgehog scowled and attempted to steer his wife forward, but she stood firm, enjoying the attention. EG watched to see if Fenella got that weird, warm feeling that she had when she first shook hands with Pink Rabbit. She couldn't tell: Fenella's cheeks flushed a little, but that could just be because Pink Rabbit was giving her so many compliments.

Still a little flustered, Fenella turned to EG, "Here my dear, some of your favourite flavours." With that, the top of her hat flipped open and a little wicker shopping basket of muffins was raised up on a small platform.

EG's face lit up as she reached for the basket. The lid of the hat instantly flipped back down. EG and Fenella grinned at each other. She then talked Fenella through her new generator, who was equally impressed and intrigued. Fenella asked technical questions, which were beyond Hedgehog, but he still nodded knowingly.

"Yes, you do need more security here. Especially as your Services grow. You've got to think about client confidentiality." Fenella looked around P.O.N.D. as she spoke. "You know I'd be very happy to help. Under your guidance of course."

"And I should be very happy to help you Fenella," added Pink Rabbit with a small bow of his head.

She nodded gracefully back and smiled.

Hedgehog then felt forced to offer his help!

"We could start on Phase 1 tomorrow. I think my other ideas will need more work," said EG.

"You should all come to ours for dinner afterwards, as the children are at their grandparents."

"Or maybe," said Hedgehog with a sly smile, "Pink Rabbit would like to have us all over to *his* house for dinner." He waited for the rabbit's excuse.

Pink Rabbit paused as everyone looked at him. He gave a relaxed smile, then said, "I should be delighted if you would all dine at my house. Thank you for such a wonderful suggestion Hedgehog."

Fenella looked proudly at her husband.

Hedgehog was taken aback: he hadn't expected this. "Well, just make sure it's not only carrot muck, that there's some proper food."

"My dear friend – this will be fine dining, the like of which you have never seen before."

Hedgehog just scowled.

Chapter 16

A Home Fit for the Grand Master of Pinkdom

Everyone arrived at P.O.N.D. the next day bright and breezy. Fenella picked a few leaves off her husband and said incredulously,

"Do you get stuck there *every time* darling? But you just need to swing your legs through like I did. And the brook is such a tiny little thing."

Hedgehog flicked his eyes at the grinning rabbit and mumbled at his wife that they'd talk about it later.

"I made up a few quick sketches of Phase 1 last night. I think this is the best way to go to camouflage the place," said EG, and she rolled out a set of the most immaculate drawings: neat, precise, architectural style drawings with different elevations and scales.

No-one said anything.

EG looked at them, a little anxious. "Err…aren't they very clear then?"

"It's not that. We're all just a bit taken aback at how amazing and skilful all these drawings are," said Fenella, pushing up her already rolled up sleeves and bending down for a clearer look.

"Oh," said EG, a bit surprised.

"When did you do these? They must have taken ages," asked Hedgehog.

"Not really. I just did them in bed last night."

"Well, you really are your mother's daughter!" exclaimed Pink Rabbit.

EG had not expected a comment like this - she didn't even think Pink Rabbit knew her mother was an architect. She just twisted her mouth, not really wanting to reply.

"Well, if you think they're clear enough." There was a unanimous agreement that that was an understatement. "Let's get started then." EG then proceeded to explain her drawings; Fenella asked the most incisive questions, clearly able to follow everything. The other two nodded in what they felt were the right places.

"I love the idea of camouflage netting round the back and sides. I assume you've got lots of netting?" asked Fenella. She stood up, adjusting her purple beret that had an unusually thick hem.

"Of course."

"Of course," smiled Fenella.

"The voice activated drawbridge to the shed particularly interests me," said Pink Rabbit. EG looked up. "However, what if someone were to try to do an impression of one of us and attempt to gain access." He then did a rather poor impression of Hedgehog.

"I do NOT sound like that!"

His wife shrugged, tilted her head and pulled an I'm-not-so-sure face. "It *could* be you."

"What! Ok then, what about 'Ooh my, pinkness!' I could easily be Pink Rabbit."

"Oh, the machine will know whether it's you," interrupted EG and continued talking more and more quickly as her enthusiasm grew. "When we talk, we make vibrations in the air. The machine will convert, or change, these into digital data – the language computers use. Then it will get rid of any background noise, so it's just your voice. Then it will work out what's your normal speed and volume. Then work out how you, individually, phrase things. So it builds up a voice picture of you, you could say!" She drew breath.

The other three listened dumbfounded.

"You never cease to amaze me with your knowledge of how things work. Can I help you? I'd love to understand more," said Fenella.

"Great. You two could put together the camouflage nets." EG nodded at Hedgehog and Pink Rabbit as she spoke.

Her two friends looked at each other. Pink Rabbit smiled; Hedgehog scowled. "The net, rope and string are all in the shed. Just follow the plan and you'll be fine."

It wasn't long before Pink Rabbit had managed to tie himself up in the net, whereas Hedgehog nimbly knotted all the nets together.

"Let me guess, with this knotty skill, you were sailing champion as well as one of diving!" asked Pink Rabbit.

"No, my grandfather taught me actually."

"That must have been nice."

Unsure whether he was being sarcastic or not, Hedgehog looked up at the rabbit, but he was looking down at his net trying to disentangle himself from it.

"I never had a grandfather myself," he continued.

Hedgehog now felt a little uncomfortable. "Oh, I'm sorry. Did they both grandfathers die before you were born?"

"No. I just never had any grandparents." He seemed to be getting more, not less, entangled in the net.

"What do you mean? Of course you did, you couldn't have had parents otherwise."

With an exasperated cry, Pink Rabbit finally got the huge net off him and, with a bounce, stood up. "Well, I did not. Or rather, not in the way that you do. You know, I think I shall gather some leaves and branches for the camouflage while you do the nets – that seems more suited to my superior intellect." And before Hedgehog could say anything, he bounced off. Hedgehog watched him for minute, confused as to what that conversation had actually meant, but was then distracted as his wife came over to admire his handiwork.

It took EG and Fenella most of the morning to solder and wire up the voice activator. By the afternoon, EG began to make the drawbridge by sawing a hotchpotch collection of wood. Once the others were free to help, it didn't take long to fit together the planks and cross-planks, with Pink Rabbit deftly hammering in nails. Fenella thoroughly enjoyed herself, loving being away from the demands of home and children.

However, it took all four of them to hoist the drawbridge up and attach it to the shed with a mixture of hinges. Finally, EG fitted the large rope and pulley system that could be operated from both inside and outside the shed.

"All we've got left to do is record our voices, that way it'll be just us who can lower the drawbridge." EG plugged the voice activator device into her laptop, as Pink Rabbit hopped off to make himself up a 'well-deserved carrot cocktail'. She tapped at her keyboard, bringing up, what seemed to Hedgehog, a random series of numbers, letters and symbols on the screen.

"Ok, Fenella you go first." EG pressed the return key.

"Helloo, this is Fenella Hedgehog, may I come in?" pronounced Fenella in her poshest voice.

"I think it might be best if you just use your normal voice," EG said gently. "And just say your name."

Fenella flustered a little, then said her name into the computer. Once EG and Hedgehog had recorded theirs, Pink Rabbit shouted over in an offhand manner, "Pink Rabbit, Grand Master of Pinkdom," then immediately wound up his clockwork blender for his cocktail.

Hedgehog sighed.

"Come on Pink Rabbit, let's see if it works," called EG, excitedly.

Putting down his cocktail, he walked over to the shut drawbridge and spoke airily into the voice pad on the side of the shed: 'Pink Rabbit, Grand Master of Pinkdom'. However, he quickly lost his casual air as the door suddenly slammed down, missing him by a whisker. He hopped back in horror. Just as he regained his balance, the drawbridge flipped back up again – down and up, down and up it went, like a wild dragon's tongue.

Panicking, EG tapped away on her laptop and finally got it to stop.

"You're probably not doing it right," said Hedgehog, who marched up to the voice pad and said "Frederich Hedgehog," masterfully. The drawbridge came down smoothly and calmly and stayed down. "Told you." He stepped back looking smug.

"Maybe," said EG. "You need to stand back and shout it cos that's how it was recorded."

Pink Rabbit dutifully stood back and shouted his name. The drawbridge eased down again. He lifted his cocktail in salute to Hedgehog.

"Right," said Hedgehog. "What about this spectacular, 'never-seen-before' meal at your house that you promised us?"

"Why yes, of course. Let us depart now."

"It'll be so nice not to have to cook," said Fenella, putting her purple beret back on, for with all the hard work, she had been forced to remove her hat for once.

Pink Rabbit chivalrously offered her his arm, which she took with a smile of thanks, and they walked on, arm in arm, with Hedgehog looking grumpy behind. EG smiled at him and put her arm through his, and his face softened immediately.

*****

"How much further?" complained Hedgehog, as he'd stomped and sweated across several muddy fields, over a couple of stiles, through unwelcoming gorse bushes and finally clambered over a very rickety fence. All the while working hard, to make it seem like he wasn't working hard, to keep up with everyone.

"Yes, I suppose it would seem far for those with short legs." Still with arms linked, Pink Rabbit patted Fenella's hand. "Not you of course Fenella, for you have such long legs." She glowed with pride and stretched out her stride a little longer.

Pink Rabbit then stopped abruptly. "We are here." They all came to a halt in the middle of a flat, yet over-grown field, seemingly neglected by farmers for years. The surrounding fields were all either full of grown crops or recently harvested.

"Where's here?" asked EG, puzzled.

Hedgehog span round 360 degrees. "Where's your *house*?"

"As I say, here!" Holding out the flat of his hand he gestured at their feet. He then bent down to pull out a circular sod of turf about the size of a large dustbin lid. Instantly, a jewel-like, amber glow radiated out, causing everyone, except Pink Rabbit, to step back in surprise. A little apprehensively, they all leaned forward and peered into the mysterious hole.

There was a single large tunnel with walls that appeared to be lined with golden silk. Dotted along the sides were small gas lamps that flickered gently, sending soft images across the walls. Ahead, EG could just make out that the tunnel split off into further passages.

"Wow!" gasped Hedgehog softly.

Pink Rabbit turned and smiled. "High praise indeed. I thank you." He held out an arm to them all and said, "Do come in."

The tunnel descended gently and was easily large enough for them all to walk upright.

"I thought rabbits made small warrens," said Fenella, allowing her fingers to caress the silk walls as she made her way along.

"Fenella, as I am sure you have long noticed, I am no ordinary rabbit. I have no wish to scurry around in the mud. I always walk proud." As he spoke, he stood very erect, in almost military fashion.

Hedgehog muttered something that EG thought was a word to replace 'proud'.

In awe, all four drifted along the silk lined tunnel as it sloped easily downwards. At the end were three further tunnels, each again lined completely in silk: a rich, vibrant red, a stunning burnt orange and a deep, hot pink. Pink Rabbit waved a hand to the pink tunnel. "That leads to my sleeping arrangements. Come this way." His large, soft feet padded gently down the rich, red tunnel; his pink fur almost red too in the glowing lamplight. After a couple of minutes, they found themselves in an extremely large circular room. EG felt like she'd walked into a magnificent Bedouin tent, as the same fabric billowed loosely from the walls. More small gas lamps adorned the walls – where there was room. Because in every conceivable space on the walls were framed photos. Photos of Pink Rabbit and all uniformly mounted in simple black frames. As EG looked more closely she could see that it was Pink Rabbit with lots of different famous people: Elizabeth I, Barack Obama, Elvis Presley, William Shakespeare, Rosa Parks – endless key people from history.

"If you will excuse me for a moment, I shall just check on the food. Please make yourselves comfortable." Pink Rabbit swung back a huge tapestry that hung from ceiling to floor and disappeared. Hedgehog looked around for somewhere to sit. There were cushions everywhere all covered in rich North African patterns and varying in sizes, but no actual seats. He plonked himself down and sank deeply into several large cushions, stretched out his arms and legs and sighed, "Ahhh."

EG and Fenella examined the photos. "Do you think they're real?" asked EG. "It'd make him dead old! But, they don't look fake."

"Of course they're fake!" said Hedgehog, without looking up. "He's always claiming he knows someone or other. If they're real, I'll eat...I'll eat my waistcoat!"

"Then eat away, my dear Hedgy!" said Pink Rabbit having just returned to the room. Hedgehog started, unaware that the rabbit was behind him. As he struggled to sit up and respond, he was thrown by Pink Rabbit's startling outfit. For he was now wearing a deep bottle green, velvet smoking jacket with a burgundy, silk cravat, both of which had the letters P.R. embroidered rather elegantly on them. The same initials were also on his black velvet moccasin slippers.

"What *have* you got on?" asked Hedgehog, incredulous."

"This," Pink Rabbit flicked his hand down his clothing, "is a standard of dress that you could only aspire to."

"It smells delicious," said Fenella, rather quickly, her silky nose twitching to the scent of food in the air. "What are we having?"

"Come through – it is ready!"

They all left the red glow of the living room and entered another extremely large circular room of burnt orange silk. EG looked closely at the fabric and noticed that it had tiny bunches of carrots embroidered in the same orange. For some reason, she felt a need to run her hand gently over them and then felt a warm sensation as she did so. Confused as to why, she turned back to the group, and just caught Pink Rabbit as he looked away from her and spoke to the others.

At the back of the room was a large range for cooking, with shelves and cupboards either side filled with exotic ingredients. Hanging from rods attached to the ceiling were bunches of carrots of all sizes and colours – black, purple, orange, yellow. Several pots were bubbling away on the range and a beautiful sweet, spicy smell graced the air.

In the centre of the room was a black, smoked glass, rectangular table, which was set with exquisite silver cutlery (which EG guessed was handmade, as her mum collected handmade silver; one hobby of her Mum's which EG actually found vaguely interesting). Linen napkins were folded into large, elegant origami rabbits, which Hedgehog immediately unravelled. And at each seat was a large silver plate, each of which had an equally large silver dome placed on top, with a smaller dome on a smaller plate to one side.

"Hmm, what are we having then?" Hedgehog started to peek under his dome. Pink Rabbit gently put a hand on top to prevent him.

"What would you like to be having?" asked Pink Rabbit.

"What?"

"I'm sure whatever it is, it will be delicious," said Fenella. "Is it a recipe from your travels?"

"What travels?" asked Hedgehog, in a voice that clearly said he doubted there'd been any travels.

"I have been sharing with your good wife my many experiences around this lovely world."

"Hmm." He replied with a face that said he didn't believe anything the rabbit said. "Anyway, it'd better not be just carrots for dinner, or some other carrot muck."

"Well, let us start then and see." Everyone took their places according to calligraphed name markers and then Pink Rabbit lifted his silver dome. On his plate was a single, black carrot.

"Oh. My. God!" exclaimed Hedgehog.

Everyone nervously lifted their own domes. EG and Fenella gasped, then laughed. Hedgehog was silent.

EG had Mexican chimichangas (she even loved the name) and home-made guacamole (chunky – not too blended). Fenella had new potatoes and freshly caught salmon, with a small dollop of caviar on the side. Under Hedgehog's dome was a juicy steak and thick cut chips, with peppercorn sauce and gently steamed asparagus tips. More to the point, they all had their favourite meals.

"How on earth did you know?" asked Fenella, completely delighted.

Pink Rabbit shrugged. "I listen."

EG couldn't speak as she had already shoved a large forkful into her mouth. It only took Hedgehog a few moments to catch her up.

They all ate and chatted and laughed. They talked about solving the mystery, the bullies, the gangplanks, and piranhas, and ideas for future mysteries.

'Dessert next,' thought Hedgehog. He sat up, looking at the small silver dome in anticipation – the main had been perfect, so this should be good! Which he obviously did not say out-loud.

However, Pink Rabbit had taken their now finished plates and had returned with very small china bowls.

Disappointed with the size of the bowl, Hedgehog peered in. On seeing the contents, particularly the bright orange colour, he screwed up his face and asked disgruntledly, "What's this stuff?"

"Carrot sorbet – it freshens up your tastebuds, cleanses the palate, preparing you for your next course. You did not think you would dine here without encountering a carrot or two?" he said with a smile.

"Mm, it's actually quite nice Hedgehog. Sweet and fresh!" EG scooped up another mouthful.

Hedgehog reluctantly dipped in the very, very edge of his spoon and tentatively put it ever so slightly into his mouth. 'Yum!' he said silently to himself. He then quietly, and yet very enthusiastically, finished off his bowl. All the time careful not to let the rabbit see he liked it. "'S'alright," he said, scraping his spoon round the bottom of the bowl for the melted remains.

"Now for dessert," declared Pink Rabbit. Everyone eagerly lifted their small silver dome, and, as everyone had now hoped, found that it was their favourite pudding. Pink Rabbit had carrot cake – "Not as good as yours Fenella, but I have tried." Indeed, it was a miniature cake, but stacked incredibly high with icing and gloriously decorated with marzipan carrots that looked so life-like. EG of course had treacle pudding *and* lemon meringue pie – huge portions. Fenella smiled happily at her baked Alaska ("so clever how the ice-cream never melts inside the cooked meringue, don't you think?"). Hedgehog looked excited and then a little embarrassed at his lavender and lime tart, lightly dusted with icing sugar. "The lavender just brings out the lime, that's all it's there for," he said quickly, as if having lavender was a bit sissy.

As Pink Rabbit showed them out at the end of the meal, they were a full and very satisfied group. Rather slowly, they made their way back up the tunnel. Hedgehog groaned a little that his stomach hurt and that it must have been the carrot sorbet. "Or maybe the extra helpings of pudding, darling," said Fenella, pushing him from behind to catch up with the others. Just as she spoke, they heard a loud scream from outside in the field above. Fenella and Hedgehog scurried out to find Joey sprawled on the ground, scrambling to stand up. Taken by surprise as EG and the others had come out of the hole in the ground, he had stumbled back and fallen.

EG rushed over to help him. Taking his hand to pull him up she said, "I've been looking out for you, I've been wanting to tell you that we've sorted out those bullies. No more worries for you," He mumbled a thanks. EG's grin suddenly dropped as she noticed fresh bruises up his arm. "What! Are they still bullying you?"

Joey yanked down his loose hoodie sleeve. "No. No!" He turned to walk off.

"Wait. What are those bruises from then? It looks like somebody's grabbed you. It better not be those girls."

"I said, it's not them."

"So, who?"

He mumbled something and again tried to walk away.

"Who?"

"My dad, ok?!"

Hedgehog was appalled. "Why don't you tell your mother?"

"Yeah, right, like she'd do anything."

"But…" Hedgehog didn't know what to say to that.

"Look, leave it ok. It doesn't matter." This time he turned and ran.

"Wait," EG tried to run after him, but he'd already cut across the fields through an opening that she'd not noticed before.

Coming back, panting a little, she asked, "What are we going to do now?"

"What do you mean?" asked Pink Rabbit.

"Well, we can't leave him to suffer at someone else's hands. No wonder he got caught up by those girls, he's probably spent the whole of his life being bullied by his parents."

"I don't think there's anything we *can* do," said Fenella gently.

"Yes, there is! I'm sure there is! We just need to think of it – don't we Pink Rabbit?" She turned to look at her friend, not quite why she was appealing to him directly, but somehow she knew he would want to help Joey.

Pink Rabbit looked into her Galaxy brown eyes, which sparkled defiantly.

"Of course you are right, we do need to help someone who is unhappy. We just need one of your infamous plans EG. What do you say Hedgy-boy?" He looked at Hedgehog.

Without hesitation, Hedgehog said firmly. "Absolutely. Let's meet up first thing tomorrow. Muffins at the ready!"

"I'll make a fresh batch for Frederich to bring in the morning," added Fenella

EG's furrowed brow gently smoothed away. It felt so good to have people she could rely on, people who saw the world as she did, people who 'got' her.

"Argh!" They all span round to see Pink Rabbit, who was lifting his feet one by one off the ground. "My beautiful silk velvet moccasins, purchased at full price! What possessed me to come outside in this swamp-like mud?" Desperately and yet rather unnecessarily, he tried to hop back across the tiny clumps of days-old-dried mud to the tunnel. "Argh, now excrement!" was the last thing the others heard as they made their way back across the fields to their own homes.

Chapter 17

An Alien Invasion

Hoping to get things ready for their planning session, EG decided to arrive early the next morning at P.O.N.D. before the other two turned up, but to her surprise they were already there. Not only that, but they had large sheets of paper out on the ground and equally large marker pens and were busy writing notes and sketching drawings. They clearly had had a few 'disagreements' as the drawings were rather messy ones with lots of crossings out, and the backs of their hands had pen marks all over them. However, as she walked up to them, they looked up and were all smiles.

"What's all this?" she asked, bending down to look at what seemed to be a pile of rubbish.

"A few items that we found on the way here – we believed that you might consider this rubb-, this *stuff*, useful."

She hadn't heard Pink Rabbit stop himself from calling it all rubbish, as she was excitedly rifling through everything. "Cool, a lawn mower blade, oh, and a squash ball – yes, this'll be useful for- ooh look! An umbrella frame!"

"And there's one trainer in that lot. *One* trainer. How can someone lose <u>one</u> and not notice?" asked Hedgehog.

"That is one mystery that we shall leave to some other detective agency to solve. Come on, EG, come see our ideas for helping Joey," said Pink Rabbit.

Hedgehog and Pink Rabbit ran through their, albeit short, list of ideas:

1. Trap the dad in an inner tube.
2. Throw the dad in the water tower.
3. Force the dad to eat carrots. ("That was my idea," said Hedgehog gleefully. "It'd get anyone to do what you asked after that!")
4. Something Else.

"Well, clearly you've been working err...hard. I think we'll go with number 4. That's your best one," said EG. "And it needs to be something...cunning. I need to think about this."

"I put the muffins from Fenella in your drawer. There's some new flavours I think," said Hedgehog.

She walked up the drawbridge to the shed, bounced on it slightly, feeling the pleasure of having made it, then went in and pulled out her air-tight muffin drawer. She drummed her fingers on her lower lip pondering over the flavours. Lemon – no, too zingy, need a quieter mind for this one. Chocolate and fudge – no, too mellow. Ah! A new flavour from Fenella, one they'd discussed: vanilla ice-cream. Perfect. Just the right combination of warmth and freshness to get her mind going. Taking it out, she knocked the drawer shut with the side of her hip and stepped back out into the dappled sunlight. The heat eased down through the overlapping branches and softly warmed her face. She slowly peeled down the edge of the muffin case, to half-way. Equally slowly, she wandered around the pond, gently nibbling round the muffin top. Every now and then she'd stop as if she'd found a solution, then shake her head and walk on. Absentmindedly, she gently pulled the case away from the sides of the muffin and worked her way down the sponge and then, without looking, plucked out the base and ate it in one clean bite. The whole time Pink Rabbit and Hedgehog simply watched, bemused.

Finally, she wiped her mouth with the back of her hand, automatically folded up the empty muffin case into a small, interlocking triangle and turned to her two friends.

"Bullies seem strong and powerful – but what are they really?"

"Stupid?" offered Pink Rabbit.

"Yes, but what else – more basic. Why do they feel a need to be powerful and controlling?"

"Because they're evil?" growled Hedgehog. Pink Rabbit looked at him and raised an eyebrow.

"Hmm, maybe some. But most because they feel power<u>less</u> – really, they're cowards. We saw that with those girls. Big One, the so-called leader, was the one who was the most scared, whereas Ginger, who didn't really seem to get involved in the bullying, was the one who faced up and got out first."

"Right," said the other two, slowly.

"So, I bet Joey's dad, because he's such a *big* bully, hurting his own child, is a <u>real</u> coward. So we need to <u>really</u> scare him. And I mean, **really** scare him."

"Right," they said slowly, again.

"If we make him believe something 'other-worldly' is threatening him and demanding that he behaves like a proper dad or it will somehow get him, I reckon he'll really fall for it."

"What you are saying is that we convince him, somehow, that something from another world is visiting him, and that he should now be nice to his son." Pink Rabbit was clearly doubtful. "Do people believe in things such as this?"

Wanting to be supportive, Hedgehog said, "People believe in all kinds of things – UFOs, little green men." And he added pointedly, "*pink* rabbits."

Pink Rabbit arched an eyebrow. "I do not require people to *believe* in me. I simply am."

Hedgehog sighed and shook his head.

EG grabbed some of the large pieces of paper, knelt down and started sketching.

"We'll need to do a recce of course. Joey's always going off past Sutton's fields so I'm sure he lives in Whight House, because that's the only house that I could see on Google Earth in that direction. Of course we'll need some kind of sound system, and maybe lights that'll fool Joey's dad enough to make our disguises convincing."

"Ooh, disguises!" said Pink Rabbit, excitedly.

"We're all different sizes," continued EG. "So that'll make the disguises more effective."

Pink Rabbit patted Hedgehog on the head patronizingly, then said, "We will need to interfere with the electrics in their house – I am sure I could do that."

"Maybe you could link up your laptop to their TV, so that the TV comes on when the dad comes into the room and sees some spooky recording that we've made," suggested Hedgehog.

"That is actually quite a brilliant idea Hedgy!"

Hedgehog pulled in his cheeks to stop himself from smiling.

"And the voice could be talking directly to the father," added Pink Rabbit.

"We could make doors slam at random," EG was really getting into it now.

As her two friends huddled round the pieces of paper on the ground and began to list out all their other ideas, EG felt life couldn't be more perfect in that moment. She glanced up and allowed the sun to wash carelessly over her face, savouring the wonderful feeling, then she too got down to business. It took them the rest of the morning to sketch and plan everything out in detail.

Fenella (wearing a leaf green, straw hat with an attached fan whishing gently near her face) visited briefly at lunchtime. She had cold meat pies for EG and Hedgehog and herself, and carrot couscous with exotic spices for Pink Rabbit. Hedgehog silently peered over at Pink Rabbit's food, who simply smiled and tucked in.

Just as she left, Fenella pointed at the plans and said, "You do realise you're unlikely to be able to connect your laptop to their TV wirelessly, don't you? Out there you'll need access to their Ethernet cables." With that, she gracefully bustled off.

EG jumped up and stared at her sketch. She slapped her forehead - Fenella was absolutely right! Hedgehog gave a knowledgeable nod, though didn't really having a clue what his wife was talking about.

The afternoon and evening were spent making all the necessary contraptions. It never ceased to amaze Hedgehog and Pink Rabbit how everything that they needed seemed to be in the shed: large sheets of plywood of varying thicknesses; green paint; different sized pulleys; ingredients for making bouncy balls; and even an array of chemicals in a range of pots all labelled with their chemical symbols. "'Nuh three', what does this contain?" asked Pink Rabbit opening the jar. "Eewuh! Has someone been to the toilet in this? Hedgy?"

"Thank you, no! And if you value your precious pinkness, you'll put that back, very carefully. It's N H three, NH3 – ammonia. You find it in wee, even 'pink' wee, and it'll take your fur off."

Pink Rabbit's eyes widened and he carefully fastened the lid.

It was quite late when they'd finally finished; there was not even time for a celebratory Fab. They were unanimous that tomorrow night would be the best time to carry out the recce.

"That will give me plenty of time to get ready," announced Pink Rabbit and hopped off home.

"What does he mean 'get ready'? What does he think we've been doing all this time? What's he up to?" asked Hedgehog, looking at EG and then after the rabbit, and back again.

EG just shrugged.

*****

If her dad was home, Saturday mornings at EG's house were often cooked breakfasts, much to her Mum's disapproval. Dad said he deserved it after a stressful week; Mum said he deserved not to turn into a human doughnut. EG was getting skilled at blocking out their bickering, she would just put up an imaginary metal grill round her mind. Useful today, as she loved these breakfasts - it was always the works: sizzling sausages and bacon, runny egg, grilled tomatoes, fried bread, mushrooms and sometimes, if she fancied it, baked beans – all with lots of mayo! Admittedly, she could hardly move afterwards and felt she wouldn't need to eat for a week. But that was fine today, as it was going to be a long night. She ignored her Mum's tuts and shakes of the head.

Anyway, thought EG, she need talk, how healthy can it be with all those chemicals on her head?

Her Mum pulled the towel round her shoulders to wipe a stray drop of hair dye from her forehead.

"What colour is it this time?" asked Dad.

EG's mum picked up the hair colour box. "'Woodland Brown'. What it really means is mid brown."

Picking up the last piece of fried bread off her plate, EG stood up. "I don't know why you always dye it different colours anyway. What's wrong with your own colour? You're always saying it's the same as mine!" She virtually spat out the last words. She then slammed the back door behind her, leaving her mother open-mouthed.

EG hadn't meant to slam it quite that hard; she felt a bit bad, but only a bit. Still seething, she just about dodged a passing car. Stomping off down Green Lane, she almost didn't see Joey. He was perched up on a high branch of Big Arm Tree. When he realised that she was looking at him he tried to hide the fact that he'd been crying.

"What?" he asked aggressively.

"Are you ok?" EG cautiously stepped forward.

"Fine," he answered sullenly.

"Is…Is it your dad again," she asked gently.

"No! Well, maybe. I don't know why I'm cr-er…upset. He's going away for a week so at least it'll be a break from everything. Me and my brother are staying at my Gran's. And maybe when he gets back, he'll be happier, cos he's trying to sell some of our land we've had for ages, and no-one's ever wanted it. So if we can get a bit of money…" His voice faded, then he quickly said, "Anyway, I'd better get home."

"You live at Whight House, don't you?"

"Yeah, why?" he looked suspicious.

"No reason." And she shrugged.

Joey jumped his gangly body down from the tree and walked off home with a single glance over his shoulder. Once out of sight, EG ran full pelt to P.O.N.D. headquarters where Pink Rabbit and Hedgehog were doing some final tweaking to the equipment.

"Must…do…it…tonight," panted EG, with her hands on her thighs.

"What?" asked Hedgehog. Pink Rabbit looked puzzled.

"No time for a recce tonight…the dad's going away tomorrow for a week…we've got to do it tonight – for real!"

"What!!" exclaimed Hedgehog and Pink Rabbit in unison.

"We need to see the place so we can set up properly," said Hedgehog.

"It'll be fine – we know what we're doing," she said.

"Okay…"

"I suppose everything is ready this end. Yes, yes, it will be much more fun to be spontaneous!" Pink Rabbit bounced around excitedly.

"Okay…," said Hedgehog again. "So we just wait till dark then?"

EG hesitated. "I did tell Fenella I'd help fix a cover for the window at your house, I may as well do that now. Then action stations tonight!" She started to walk off, checking the potential wind velocity for tonight on an App that she'd written for her phone.

Hedgehog looked at EG and then at Pink Rabbit. "I'll come with you," he said quickly and scampered after her.

Pink Rabbit gave them a careless wave as he had already started making a carrot cocktail, before he got down to some serious snoozing.

****

"Ssh!" snapped Hedgehog. "Stop grunting!"

"I am ghostly quiet! And excuse me, I do not grunt! I am making my normal delicate breathing noises, even though these items are awfully heavy!" The three of them finally made it to Joey's house, laden with all their equipment. Sheets of painted wood were strapped to the already bulging wheelbarrow; their backpacks sprouting equipment and tools.

As an intensely white full moon emerged from behind rolling clouds, Hedgehog looked aghast at Pink Rabbit.

"And what are you wearing?" asked Hedgehog in disbelief.

Pink Rabbit was dressed in a black roll neck jumper, with a black army flak jacket on top. In the pockets, where weapons would normally be slotted, were several protruding carrots and an antique fob watch on a chain. He also sported black combat trousers but in a strange tweed-like material and a black ski mask. However, the part of the mask that was supposed to go over his mouth was actually tucked under his chin and his ears were sticking out of holes in the top, though admittedly they were smeared with black camouflage paint. A pair of night vision goggles were strapped to his forehead and a periscope slung over his shoulder.

"I am appropriately dressed for the mission ahead, that is all."

"So, that's what you meant earlier about getting ready!"

"After that incident with the sheep excrement, I said I would never be ill-prepared again. And anyway, we agreed to dress in black."

"Yeah, but there's dressing in black for camouflage, and there's, well, what you've got on."

To blend into the dark night, EG had on a black hoodie and black jeans. Hedgehog was wearing a black waistcoat with a black army style beret. He then sniffed the air. "Are you wearing perfume too?!"

"Thank you for noticing. It is a gentle fragrance that I thought might make the night more pleasant." Hedgehog tutted and shook his head.

They crouched low behind the hedge that bordered the front garden; the house looked desolate, isolated, amidst deathly black fields.

"I can't believe anyone actually lives here – it's a ruin," said Hedgehog. A single, stone house painted a cold, pale blue stood before them, a ramshackle vision barely held together. Two rusty bikes and a mouldy old mattress cowered in the overgrown grass, which spilled out across a cracked footpath that led to the front door.

"I have seen worse," said Pink Rabbit, sombrely.

As he spoke, a tile slid from the roof and crashed to the steps outside the front door.

They all quickly ducked even lower behind the hedge. EG looked desperately at their pile of equipment that was still visible from the house. They all held their breath waiting for someone to burst out of the front door. After a few moments, Pink Rabbit carefully raised his periscope over the hedge and whispered, "I do not think our plan has been foiled."

Dark clouds moved menacingly overhead, swallowing the moon.

"Right, one of us needs to creep up to the living room window and check if they've gone to bed yet. There's lights on, but that could mean they've just forgotten to turn them off."

Silence, as her two friends continued to look at her.

"Ok," said EG. "<u>One</u> of us. Who?"
Silence.
"Hedgehog, what about you?"

"Seconded," said Pink Rabbit quickly. "Right, you are on, Hedgy-boy."

"You could roll up there quite discretely," encouraged EG.

"You would be like a ball of ninja-ness – with marvellous beret," added Pink Rabbit, with a wry smile and twiddling the 'tail' on top of Hedgehog's beret.

"Ok, ok," grumbled Hedgehog, smacking the rabbit's hand away. "But use those things and keep an eye on me." He pointed to Pink Rabbit's night-vision goggles, which he now brought down over his eyes.

"Roger-dodge Hedgy. Off you go!"

He shrugged off his backpack and with deftness and ease, rolled himself up into a tight ball, then propelled himself towards the living room window. He stopped precisely three centimetres from the wall and unfurled himself. Unfortunately, he couldn't quite see over the windowsill into the room. He looked round at his friends, hands out questioningly. A be-goggled Pink Rabbit pointed animatedly to a large flowerpot to Hedgehog's right. As quietly as he could, he upturned it and stood on it to peer in through the window. As he stepped off, the pot began to topple and wobble. Hedgehog, eyes wide with horror, launched himself forwards, arms out and grabbed it - *just*.

EG frantically waved for him to return.

Having rolled equally smoothly back to his friends, he panted, "No-one's there. Cos the door was open, I could see into other rooms. Looks clear."

"Right, we'll get in the house first and set everything up," said EG. They all shrugged their backpacks more comfortably onto their backs and stealthily made their way to the front door. As he still had the night-vision goggles on, Pink Rabbit couldn't see immediately in front of himself, so he kept tripping up and banging into Hedgehog. Exasperated, Hedgehog stopped, turned and yanked the goggles down off the rabbit's eyes. Once at the door, EG pulled out a small canvas wallet and unfurled it. Inside were a range of thin, metal picks with varying ends – zigzags, curves, serrations. She pulled out one of the smallest and quickly picked the lock.

"Where did you get *those*?" whispered Hedgehog.

"I made them yonks ago – I've been dying to try them out for real," she answered excitedly. The door opened with a gentle click.

Once inside, they all moved in different directions, all with purpose. EG couldn't see what the other two were doing, but she knew they would follow the agreed plans to the last detail. She moved silently herself, gagging a little from the ugly stench of stale cigarette smoke that clung to the air. She noted two large suitcases standing in the hall – the parents were clearly packed and ready for tomorrow.

Just as she had nearly finished all the tasks that she had been assigned, she heard dull footsteps. She tensed. Then melted back into the shadows. As the steps drew closer, she checked her body for some kind of weapon, finding only a roll of sticky-back plastic tucked in her tool belt. With a white knuckled grip, she held it above her head. Teeth gritted. She was ready! On the verge of swinging the plastic roll, she relaxed her arm at the last moment. Pink Rabbit and Hedgehog appeared, shoving each other forward, their backpacks now considerably lighter.

"You unlocked the back door?" she whispered.

Hedgehog nodded.

"What are you doing?" asked Pink Rabbit quietly, as EG had turned to the front door and whipped out a screwdriver from her back pocket.

"A 'bonus item' that I've only just thought of." Within moments, she screwed the doorbell back in place.

"Come on EG," urged Hedgehog. "We need to get a move on. They could wake up at any moment."

They all sprinted back to the front gate and, with great care, pushed the wheelbarrow down the side path to the back of the house. It ran smoothly over the ground, thanks to the supersize wheels EG had put on. Truly cross-terrain. EG paused briefly to disable the huge monster of a satellite dish on the side of the house. Once in the back garden, they knew that this was the hard bit of the set-up. All three quickly worked up a sweat, even Pink Rabbit. Though he did keep stopping to pat his forehead down with a black silk handkerchief. With this part of their plan erected, they moved silently to see to the last few items.

"You two are staying at the back as agreed, yeah?" They nodded. "Pink Rabbit you'll need to start making the rubber ball mix now, so that the consistency's just right."

Silently, he pulled out a packet from his backpack, like an archer pulling an arrow from his quiver, and nodded.

EG stole back round the front of the house and entered through the living room window, which she had left slightly ajar. She pressed play on the stereo remote control – her pre-recorded CD that she'd put in their old stereo began to play. A great rumbling and throbbing resonated throughout the house. Yes, she thought, it sounds perfect. She'd guessed they wouldn't have anything more high-tech than a stereo. She slid back out the front window, old paint flaking off as she did so, and pushed it almost to behind her. Crouching down beneath the ledge, she picked up her waiting laptop. She knew Pink Rabbit and Hedgehog would have taken the sounds as their cue. She didn't have to wait long before she heard a male voice spitting out expletives and then a thud of feet coming down the threadbare stairs. Joey's father yanked open the living room door. EG knew he wouldn't notice the stereo as she'd blacked out the lights on it. Suddenly the black screen of their incredibly large flat-screen TV came alive with a single huge word: 'STOP!'

Joey's dad halted abruptly. "What?!" His bulging belly shook slightly as it oozed out of his food-stained, once-white vest.

Sitting outside, below the window, EG quickly typed 'STOP' again on to her laptop. Once more the word STOP flashed up on the TV.

The bleary-eyed man looked nervously round the room, peering tentatively behind the large black, pleather settee.

This time EG typed: WE ARE HERE TO MAKE YOU STOP!

"Who are you? What yer playin' at?" shouted Joey's dad, jutting out a large stubbled chin, trying to sound braver than he felt.

EG typed in a quick command and both sets of curtains in the living room began to open and close, open and close, swishing furiously. She then pressed the CD player remote control and high-pitched squeaks filled the room. She now typed: MY FRIENDS AGREE, YOU MUST STOP THE EVIL THAT YOU ARE DOING TO YOUR CHILDREN

"What?" he spluttered at the TV. "Evil? Rubbish! I love my kids. I'm a great dad."

Annoyed, EG turned the high-pitched squeaks louder until the walls almost vibrated. The dad span round, desperately searching for the source. But EG had hidden tiny speakers everywhere, so that it was difficult to tell where the sound was actually coming from. Reluctantly, she turned the volume down again.

"What are they saying?" he asked the TV anxiously. He suddenly lunged forward and ripped the TV's plug from the socket, then pulled his back sharply in to avoid the curtains, which continued to slide back and forth angrily.

IF YOU DO NOT STOP WE WILL SHOW YOU EVIL. EG was pleased that the battery pack she'd fitted to the back of the TV had kicked in. She'd known he'd try and pull the power. The cheap curtains chose now to jam, but they still twitched eerily.

Joey's father backed carefully to the doorway, stunned that the TV continued to work. "You don't scare me," he stammered. He then turned his fat body to the door to escape, but before he could the door slammed as if an invisible force had made it happen. Hearing the crash of wood on wood, EG smiled. She knew Pink Rabbit had pulled it to with string attached to a pin at the bottom of the door. The string would have been released as he pulled, so there would be no evidence. She hoped they wouldn't stand on the pin – well, maybe the dad, she grinned to herself.

Now panic-stricken, Joey's father launched his bulk of a body towards the door and banged his fists on it repeatedly. He then reached to yank hard on the door, thinking it would be locked; caught unawares that it wasn't, he tumbled heavily to the floor. Moving like a hefty walrus on land, he tried to get to his feet. He looked up to see his wife shuffling nervously downstairs, a grubby, baby blue nightie with the slogan 'I'm Gorgeous' enveloped her like the skin of a fat sausage. "W-what's going on?" she pulled her tatty pink dressing gown firmly shut, hugging herself.

EG left the chest-vibrating pulses playing while she sprinted round to the back of the house.

"There's something here – I think it's out the front," he answered, his eyes darting round.

"What d'you mean there's something here? What's making that noise?"

"I – I think it's aliens."

"Don't be stupid! What is it?" Her voice trembled and she took an anxious step backwards.

Looking round, he grabbed his wife. "Come on, we've got to get out of 'ere," They ran, as fast as their fat bodies would allow, to the door to the kitchen and pushed it hard. As it opened, they screamed – a scream of both terror and panic. Looking down at themselves they saw they were now covered in green slime, that oozed and gunged down their bodies.

"Maybe it's a ghost!" screeched Joey's mum. "This is ectoplasm! Oh my God!"

In the back garden, the three P.O.N.D. detectives were poised, having heard the wailing. Even in the dark, Pink Rabbit could see EG's look of intense focus and cool determination. He knew she would try her utmost to make this plan work. But there was something else in those dark eyes which made him wonder how far she would go. Would she stop at nothing?

Still yelling and screaming, the husband and wife panicked and desperately tried to flick off the slime. Then Joey's Dad gasped and stepped clumsily back into his wife.

"Look!" With a shaking hand, he pointed to their greasy oven. The light of the oven clock, which was normally numbers, now read STOP in bright red lights.

His wife backed away from the oven, "Stop? Why 'Stop'?" the fear in her voice rising uncontrollably. Then she felt a sudden whoosh of cool air on her back. She swivelled round with a start, her grimy dressing gown falling open. Her back had almost touched the fridge door, which for some reason stood slightly ajar. From within, came a light, not the normal fridge light, but an incredibly bright green light. With a nervous glance at each other, they crept forwards to peer in. They slowly pulled open the door. Instantly, a luminous green lumpy sludge was catapulted sharply into their faces.

"Aargh! It's on me! It's on me!" shrieked the wife, as it slopped down her.

Her husband could barely speak as the sludge had filled his mouth. His face contorted from fear and utter disgust, as the taste was horrendous, like rotting meat and the bottom of a dustbin truck.

Outside, the three friends grinned. Everything was going to plan. EG had rearranged the bulbs in the oven light to spell out 'stop' and Pink Rabbit had fitted a spring catapult that was released when the fridge door was pulled open.

"The animal innards worked well then?" whispered Hedgehog with a grin. It had been his job to set up the 'ectoplasm', which was really lots of animal intestines that they'd got from the village butcher. He'd mixed them with luminous green paint and attached them above the kitchen door in a thin bag that would burst as the door opened. He was clearly pleased with his part of the plan so far.

EG gestured to Pink Rabbit to be ready. With quiet efficiency, he poured two pots of liquid into a prepared wooden frame in front of the backdoor: one pot of cornflour, borax and water, and another of quick setting glue. Mixing them together furiously, as he knew it wouldn't take long to set, he hoped these ingredients for making bouncy balls would work here as planned. He then hopped purposefully back to the other two and they all put on their disguises: overlarge, green, oval heads, with bulbous black eyes and tight, green rubber jumpsuits. Hedgehog, despite having practised getting into his specially adapted suit, still struggled. But slapped away the helping hand from the rabbit, nonetheless.

Eagerly, EG turned to their stores – they were now on to one of her favourite parts of the plan. She bent and picked up her remote control, World War Two aeroplane, which was covered in a puppet-like alien. It was a bomber plane that was loaded with rather different 'bombs'. Hedgehog had his hand hovering at the ready over a collection of switches which were linked to an electrical control box that EG had rigged up. Behind the three of them was a large shadow, which EG was looking forward to bringing into their plan.

The husband and wife, still yowling, scrambled to the backdoor.

"Now!" whispered EG. Hedgehog flicked one of the switches and Pink Rabbit flipped open a box by his feet and started to waft huge clouds of dry ice towards the door. The back door flew open and EG nodded at Hedgehog for him to flick another switch. Instantly eight large torches each with 1000 candle strength, all aimed at the back door, came on in an avalanche of light. Joey's parents screamed, holding their hands up in front of their eyes in a vain attempt to see. But the light was too bright – they were immobilised. They hadn't even noticed the rubber mixture beneath their feet, which now set rapidly and firmly. EG smiled wryly to herself.

With a faltering voice, Joey's dad spoke to the space in front of him, still unable to see. "Who are you? What d'yer want?" His whole body seemed to be trembling.

The three detectives stood facing their enemies, dressed in their green Area 51 alien costumes. EG was conscious of her 'head' slipping and she could hardly see out of the small hidden eye holes. Behind her, stood large and bold looming out of the shadows, cut out of plywood and propped up by a wooden frame, was their 'spaceship'. EG had got the idea from movie sets where buildings were really just the front painted onto massive sheets of wood, made to look like the whole building. With the glaring lights and atmospheric dry ice she hoped everything looked realistic.

By now, Joey's mother was whimpering, stubby arms gripping her husband. EG put on her best alien voice (she loved doing voices). Hedgehog added a few alien cheeps and gurgles as she spoke, just for good measure.

"We have come to stop your evil!"

The mother looked at her husband. "What does it mean? We don't do anything." Her voice trembled badly.

"We have seen your treatment of your sons," continued EG. "We watch you." Joey's mother gasped; her hand flew to her mouth. "You must treat them with kindness and respect." EG launched the 'bomber' alien and it zipped towards the parents, who eyed it very nervously.

"I tell you we don't do nuffin' to our kids!" shouted the dad, with false bravado.

EG could hear Pink Rabbit mutter something about an atrocious double negative.

"If you refuse, we will seek revenge on their behalf." EG flew the disguised plane a little closer, allowing it to hover over their heads.

"That one's going to get us! It's getting us!" shrieked the mother, pointing at what she thought was an alien. They tried to move their feet to escape, but the bouncy ball mixture had now become the consistency of very sticky chewing gum. Looking down at their feet, they screamed again.

Really enjoying impersonating an alien, EG shouted further demands whilst Hedgehog put in suitable other-worldly noises. "Agree to stop!"

"But, but…" stammered the mother.

EG flicked a switch on her remote control and the hovering 'alien' opened its flaps on its undercarriage, but instead of releasing bombs, out tumbled mounds of worms that had been dipped in luminous green (EG had been adamant that it should be non-toxic, so that the worms could survive happily afterwards!). She could hear her friends quietly snigger as the already grossly covered husband and wife frantically tried to bat the worms off their heads.

"It's alien stuff – it's probably poisonous!" yelled Joey's mother.

The couple tried to wriggle free - they twisted and turned, and even tried swearing but they were stuck fast. Finally, with a loud suction sound, the dad's feet popped out; he turned to run back inside.

"Don't you dare leave me!" his wife screeched, still wriggling and still desperately flicking off worms.

Her husband hesitated a moment, then reluctantly turned back and yanked her aggressively out of the rubber mixture. They waddled quickly back into the house and to the hallway to try and make a getaway out the front door.

"Pink Rabbit," said EG. "You follow them and we'll go round the front down the side of the house.

My doorbell trick only works once and then trips out, so we'll have to hurry. Oh, and take a torch to shine in their faces so they can't see you properly."

Having made it to the hall, Joey's parents grabbed their suitcases and the dad reached for the front door as his wife clung to him, whilst throwing urgent glances back over her shoulder. As soon as his hand touched the door, both their bodies jangled and shook violently, as if caught in an earthquake – they gave out screams of pain and surprise. With effort, Joey's dad wrenched his hand away from the front door latch.

"What was that?" quailed his wife.

Hidden in the shadows behind them, Pink Rabbit realised what EG had been doing earlier: she must have rewired the bell to the latch in order to give off an electric shock to whoever touched it. He suddenly felt concerned that they would get away, as EG had said the electric shock would trip out after one use. What should he do? They were going to get away. EG wanted them to promise to stop bullying their children. It was now or never.

Just as the dad was tentatively reaching for the door once more, Pink Rabbit lifted his arms and removed his fake alien head.

On their haunches, poised low beside the front door, EG and Hedgehog were ready to make their final attempt to frighten the parents into submission. They could hear the parents scuffling towards the door, hoping to escape. EG gave Hedgehog a curt nod to confirm that she was ready. He nodded crisply back. Two military commandoes ready for action.

Then EG froze. A scream. The like of which she'd never heard before.

A fireball of sound burst from Joey's parents, ripped through the deathly quiet air and enveloped her. The fear the man and wife emitted was so overwhelming. She didn't know people could even be that afraid.

At the same time, through the gaps round the door, surged the most intense white light. It had an almost unearthly quality to it. It lasted moments, but the ferocity with which it flared had made her screw up her eyes in protection. As she dared open them, she was so dazzled that dark spots swam before her eyes.

It all lasted seconds but felt like minutes. Once she'd regained her vision, EG realised, with surprise, that she now felt an incredible sense of calm and peace. The scream showed a fear she'd never known, but the feeling within *her* now was quite the opposite. A lightness flowed gently through her body and her constant desire to make the world a better a place was gone. Like an itch that always had to be scratched, but now gone. It was as if she'd finally found what she'd been looking for in her life, but didn't even know she needed. Almost immediately, however, she could feel it dissipate. She tried to keep hold of the wonderful feeling, but it trickled away like water through fingers. Looking up, she was half aware of Hedgehog still twitching oddly. It took her a few moments to register that the front door had been thrown open and Joey's parents were staggering from the house, each dragging a suitcase behind them.

"We'll stop! Honest! Just leave us alone!" The husband and wife whimpered and blundered down the garden path into the darkness.

Hedgehog made to run after them, shouting, "EG – come on!"

Unruffled, Pink Rabbit walked serenely out of the house, alien head tucked casually under his arm.

EG, now feeling more herself, stepped towards him. "What *was* that? What just happened?" She looked at him intently, oblivious to the cool night air brushing lightly across her face.

He turned to her, a gentle quizzical look on his face. "What do you mean?" For the first time since they met, EG felt an edge between them.

Hedgehog, only having got as far as the gate, as the parents had screeched away in their car, was now walking breathlessly back up the path. Heaving off his large alien head, his fur hot and sweaty, and spines askew, he asked "Why didn't you chase them EG?"

Hardly hearing her friend's question, she pressed Pink Rabbit again. "The light…" She looked directly into Pink Rabbit's inky black eyes, hoping for some kind of clue. "What was that bright light?"

"It was my torch – I shone it right at them, as you proposed. I think I managed to truly scare the hebejebbes out of them!"

EG grabbed the torch from his hand. At first the switch wouldn't work then, after several frustrated attempts, it shone brightly. She snapped round and whipped the beam back and forth across the garden. Like a theatrical spotlight it cleanly highlighted everything it fell upon: the deteriorating furniture having been long dumped outside; the overgrown weeds swallowing what few flowers remained; the gate hanging forlornly by one hinge.

"That is powerful – cool!" said Hedgehog.

"No," snapped EG, flicking the beam around the shadowy bushes and trees, creating eerie shadows behind. "This is normal torch bright, but the light that I saw was much brighter than this. You saw it too Hedgehog."

"Well, no, not really," said Hedgehog apologetically. "I couldn't see much out of this alien head, and when they screamed – phew! I think I just screwed up my eyes, cos the sound went right through you, didn't it?"

"But…but…it was so bright, as if it was, well, an alien light." She looked at Pink Rabbit imploringly.

He and Hedgehog laughed. "It is a full moon tonight and it does keep flitting in and out from behind the clouds, causing sudden brightness," Pink Rabbit offered.

"No," said EG desperately. "And anyway, you could 'feel' it, the light." She was now totally confused.

"What do you mean 'feel' it? Was it hot?" asked Hedgehog, frowning.

"It felt…'good'." She didn't want to say more than that – to say it made her whole world seem 'right'. That seemed a bit too embarrassing, just from a light. "I saw you feel it too Hedgehog. You were still, then you moved jerkily."

Hedgehog looked sheepish. "Oh that. I had a bit of, er, an itch, on er, my behind. And it was tricky to, er, see to in this costume."

Pink Rabbit roared with laughter, thoroughly delighted. "Your what?!" He peered round Hedgehog trying to see his bottom. "You do not get many superheroes who are halfway through saving the day having to stop because they have got an itchy bottom! Excellent my dear Hedgy, excellent. I shall enjoy remembering this moment." He then turned to EG. "Come on, EG, do not worry about the light, it was nothing, the torch or whatever. The important thing is we scared the parents and saved the day." He winked at Hedgehog. "We had better get all this stuff cleared up before they return and work out what really happened." He put a companionable arm around Hedgehog and they walked round the corner of the house to the back garden. EG could hear Hedgehog saying indignantly, "But it happens! Everyone gets an itch there at some point."

She flicked the torch on and off again, still unconvinced. No, it had definitely not been this. Stepping tentatively into the house, she stopped in the shabby hallway taking in her surroundings. Doors to the adjoining rooms gaped open, green gunge smeared the peeling wallpaper and rucked up carpet. She could hear the other two now in the back garden, bickering, accompanied by clatters of wood, as they took down the 'spaceship'. EG placed her hand flat on the wall. It felt cold. Had she expected it to be warm? But it hadn't been a hot light like a fire. Rather, a searing, white brightness. That wouldn't leave a warmth behind - would it? She moved into the living room, standing just inside the threshold. Her eyes pushed round the room looking for evidence of what she knew she'd seen. But as she could find no clues, her belief in it began to slip away. Maybe she had been wrong. Maybe it had been the adrenalin pumping round her body, heightening her senses. That's what they say happens, don't they? And yet, she <u>had</u> seen it. Had felt it.

Reluctantly, she knelt down, knowing she had to finish the job at hand. She slowly turned her small screwdriver, then methodically wound up all the thin wires that she'd so eagerly put in place earlier. Then packed them neatly, reel by reel, into her backpack, ready to be stored in her shed and used again some day.

Chapter 18

The End of the Beginning

It took them quite a while to gather up their equipment and clear up all their mess – especially the animal innards (which Pink Rabbit did with a very long stick and Hedgehog did holding it very close to Pink Rabbit's face). The worms had wriggled away of their own accord. The bouncy ball mixture was easy to peel off the ground now that it had set properly: it came up as a large rectangular rubber mat. When thrown, it seemed to slither in large arcs, rather than bounce, much like a seal returning to sea. Pink Rabbit and Hedgehog had a bit too much fun seeing who could make it 'slither' the furthest, like they were skimming stones across the water. "Ooh, five slithers, good one!" called Hedgehog after Pink Rabbit had done a particularly effective throw. EG had to come round and get them re-focused.

"Mind you," she said, picking the mat up. "I'm sure it'll come in useful for something one day." She flopped it up and down in her hands, mentally listing possible uses.

"I no longer require these EG, you can no doubt make use of them." Pink Rabbit held out his night-vision goggles. She took them as carefully as if she'd been handed the crown jewels, and, with fingertips, gently lowered the strap over her shoulder.

As she worked, she kept putting the goggles to her eyes and transforming her surroundings into lurid green images, just for the pure pleasure of it.

When they were finally done clearing up, they heaved the cart full of remaining equipment back round to the front of the house. Pausing momentarily, they looked back at the unloved building.

"Well, that 'mystery' is well and truly solved," said Hedgehog with a satisfied grin.

EG nodded. "Yeah. It feels good that we followed the mystery right through to the end and solved *everything*. It wouldn't have been fair to Joey to just leave it half done. Now he and his brother can come home from their Gran's and have parents who treat them like parents are supposed to."

They all felt that sleep would now be very welcome, despite the fact that the sun was beginning to show signs of daybreak. A candy floss pink feathered the sky and there was a gentle haziness to the landscape, allowing them to make out the way ahead. Hedgehog gave the wheelbarrow a big shove to get it rolling and all three manoeuvred it along back towards P.O.N.D. "You are pushing, aren't you?" Hedgehog kept asking Pink Rabbit, suspiciously. "Yes of course," always came the reply from a very relaxed rabbit.

As they neared the hedge of Garnham's Field Number Three (named ingeniously by EG and Hedgehog because it was Farmer Garnham's third largest field) close to Pink Rabbit's burrow, Pink

Rabbit said, "I shall help you return the barrow back to P.O.N.D., though quite frankly I am so tired now that I could sink immediately into a slumber, even without my luxury, ultra-lightweight, moulded eye mask!" He stretched into a yawn, his still blackened ears drooping a little. As he did so he looked up. "Ah, even the sky knows what colour to be when success is in the air."

Hedgehog took in the soft pink sky overhead. "Humph," was all he could muster.

They drew up to the gap in the hedge between Garnham's field and Pink Rabbit's when Pink Rabbit stopped abruptly; his body tensed, yawn forgotten.

"Oh my God!" gasped EG.

"Oh, Pink Rabbit…" began Hedgehog, not able to find words beyond that.

In a flash, Pink Rabbit dropped everything and bounded forward faster than EG had ever seen him move before; almost effortlessly, gliding through the air. The field had always been overgrown and forgotten - years of neglect, perfect for Pink Rabbit to make his discrete and private home. Now, however, it was freshly ploughed. All around, deep trenches were gouged, as if the quality of the earth was being assessed. Some of these deep trenches had been haphazardly refilled. Pink Rabbit came to a halt in front of a rough mass of earth and stood, motionless, staring down, oblivious to the clumps of mud that now mottled his fur.

After a moment of shock, EG ran after Pink Rabbit as fast as she could manage. Her trainers gathered thick clumps of soggy mud with every stride, so she was forced to lift her knees higher and higher just to clear each foot off the ground. Her cheeks felt the cold lines of tears, but she was unaware of it. She did feel the sharp pain in her heart – she'd never experienced a pain like that before, so just assumed it was because she was running so hard. All she knew for certain was that Pink Rabbit's home was destroyed and that she had to get to him. She pulled up sharply, finally by his side, only vaguely aware of Hedgehog behind her. With his short legs, he was struggling through the mud, tumbling then clambering to stand up. But nothing was going to stop him.

"Pink Rabbit…," began EG, half holding out a hand to comfort him. But then let it drop, feeling that whatever she'd meant to offer wasn't going to be enough. Everywhere she looked was a mangled mess of her friend's belongings. Some on the surface of the mud, some half-submerged, leaving further belongings presumably beneath the roughly discarded mass of earth. Broken fragments of cooking utensils, photos frames, clothing and lanterns lay forlornly around them, like the remnants of an air-crash. The vibrant hues of the silk fabric shreds against the dark brown, jagged mud only added to the desperate nature of the sight around EG. She felt like the damaged vibrancy *was* Pink Rabbit. Slowly, Pink Rabbit bent down to pick up a framed photo jutting out by his feet and, after considering the image for a moment, carefully brushed away the shards of broken glass.

EG made to step forward. "Pink Rabbit please don't cry, we'll…" but she couldn't finish her sentence.

"Do not worry, Pink Rabbits are not prone to crying," he said, almost distractedly, without looking up from the picture.

"Now…this…is…*maybe* …one…you…did…meet," panted Hedgehog, finally having made it across the field. He nodded to the person in the photo that Pink Rabbit was holding – Gandhi, one of India's greatest leaders, who believed a better world could be achieved through peaceful means.

Pink Rabbit raised his eyes to look at his friend, a wry smile appearing on his face. "Yes, *maybe*." He half lowered his gaze to the photo then turned back to Hedgehog, whose spines were thickly covered with mud, making him look not so much a snowball as a mudball. "Nice coat." But as Pink Rabbit made this comment without the usual tone of sarcasm, Hedgehog simply opened his mouth and closed it, unsure what to say next.

Something then made Pink Rabbit look up. "Ah, Fenella!"

All three looked to see Fenella running determinedly towards them, a pair of binoculars banging against her chest. She moved with surprising speed, with hardly any mud sticking to her. She didn't notice that her straw hat, tied with pale pink ribbon under chin, blew off her head and bobbed on her back as she ran.

She was soon by their sides. Without hesitation, she gave Pink Rabbit an enormous, heart-felt hug. "Oh, Pink Rabbit!"

Hedgehog bristled a little and started to pick the mud off his spines.

"Oh, Pink Rabbit," she continued. "As soon as I saw you all, I knew something must be wrong. I've been watching with these." She held up her binoculars. "EG let me borrow them. I needed to know that you'd all got back safely and weren't arrested or something! Oh, your home!" She turned desperately towards the scene. Then paused as if some decision had moved through her whole body. She stood tall and said very firmly, "Right, let's see what we can salvage. EG, you must have some shovels in that wheelbarrow of yours – I know you're always prepared for anything." EG nodded, and quickly ran back to the gap in the hedge where they'd left their equipment.

"Come on," Fenella pushed up her already rolled up sleeves, hitched up her skirts slightly and knelt down and began unearthing items, brushing off clumps of mud and forming a pile of belongings. Hedgehog followed suit. Pink Rabbit looked at them for a moment. It was not clear what he was thinking, but then he was down beside them, clawing mud away, burrowing down, seemingly oblivious to his 'pinkness' now.

Once EG returned with a couple of shovels it still took them a further two hours till they felt they'd recovered all that they could. Finally, they all eased their bodies up and stretched their aching backs.

"You know," said Hedgehog. "I reckon this was the field belonging to Joey's dad. He said his dad had been trying to sell it and that he'd now ploughed it up after all these years." The others simply shrugged, too tired to care.

"I think we got quite a bit and I reckon all your actual photos – not the frames obviously; they're mostly smashed. But having the photos is good, isn't it?" EG looked hopefully at Pink Rabbit.

"Yes, that is good," he replied flatly. "Yet, it does not matter how much we have recovered. It has shown me the futility of putting too much stock into belongings. It is not what we own, but who we are that is important."

"Doesn't matter how much we've recovered!" spluttered Hedgehog, mud smudged across his face and clogging his spines. "You could have told us that two hours ag-," But Fenella nudged her husband to be quiet.

"Yes," agreed Fenella. "Who we are, and having people who we love, and who love us, is much more important." She hugged Pink Rabbit again. Hedgehog shuffled his feet and grimaced, desperately wanting to comment.

EG caught the odd expression on Pink Rabbit's face, which was perhaps guilt. She frowned as to why he'd be feeling guilty now. "Why don't I go and empty the wheelbarrow back at P.O.N.D. and come back with it, load up all your stuff and then we can easily take it to…?" she faltered, as she was unable to think where to take it – the P.O.N.D.? Somewhere to make a new burrow?

But Fenella finished her sentence for her: "Our house!" she said firmly.

"What?!" spluttered Hedgehog again, almost falling over.

"What?!" exclaimed Pink Rabbit, in surprise. Hedgehog and Pink Rabbit looked at each other. Pink Rabbit, head on one side, smiling. Hedgehog aghast.

"Yes, our house," she repeated just as emphatically. Turning fully to Pink Rabbit, she said, "You must stay with us for as long as you need to."

"Why Fenella, if you are sure," said Pink Rabbit, looking delighted, then arching an eyebrow at Hedgehog.

"No she is NOT sure!" answered her husband.

"Yes I am." Fenella turned now to her husband and planted her muddy hands on her hips. "Our friend is homeless. Most of his belongings are in tatters. Are you suggesting that we turn him away?"

Hedgehog mumbled very quietly, "Yes." But shrugged, knowing it was going to happen anyway.

"You know what," said EG, suddenly inspired. "Why don't I build an extension to P.O.N.D.? You could live there – it'll be much safer than a new burrow in another field. It'll be a kind of Pink Rabbit annex."

"A Pink Rabbit Annex. Now that would be most suitable for The Grand Master of Pinkdom!" enthused Pink Rabbit.

"Oh God," said Hedgehog, hand to his forehead. "That's going to take *ages* to build." But no-one was listening.

"Right, excellent, that's settled then. Pink Rabbit will be our guest until his new home is built," decided Fenella. "Let's get everyone home. I'd ask you for breakfast my dear," she said to EG. "But I'm sure your mother will get worried if she notices you're not in bed."

The sun had now clearly risen. The muted yellow spread strongly across the horizon, enveloping the remaining wisps of pink.

EG frowned. "I shouldn't think so," she muttered. Then a bit louder to the others, "Yeah, I'd better get home before I'm missed – they'll all be up soon."

After dropping everything at P.O.N.D. and then returning for Pink Rabbit's rather sad looking pile of belongings, EG finally waved goodbye to Fenella, Hedgehog, and of course Pink Rabbit, all standing outside the green front door of Frederich and Fenella's home. The children had woken up and were already gathering around Pink Rabbit. As EG walked away she could hear young voices saying, "Really?! He's staying! Oh, this is going to be sooo cool! Isn't it Dad?...Dad?"

EG turned away from them. She was now too far away to see Hedgehog's expression, but she could picture it very clearly in her mind's eye. She smiled to herself at the thought. Despite the differences between them, and there were many, she knew absolutely how much she loved being with both Hedgehog and Pink Rabbit. These last few weeks they'd made her life full again. It was nice having people that you could trust and who appreciated you. And yes, she believed both of them really cared about her too. That felt good. Really good.

It also felt good knowing that they'd helped Mr Cuttlewell, and of course, Joey. You can't just solve a mystery, she thought, you have to look behind it, look deeper, and follow the many threads. There are always reasons for things. Joey wasn't a bad person, he'd just been forced to be a person he didn't want to be, to hide his true self. She could understand that. EG climbed the stile into Green Lane, resisted the urge to climb up Big Arm Tree, and instead headed for home.

Her mind was now buzzing with ideas for the 'Pink Rabbit Annex'. She'd try out some of the ideas she'd had for a while – it'd be brilliant fun! And it'd be great having Pink Rabbit actually live there. Being there all the time. She couldn't wait.

EG was also looking forward to seeing what P.O.N.D.'s next mystery would be. Ooh, she should check their website for messages, maybe there was one waiting…

The End

The Thank You Page

I truly feel grateful to all the people who have helped me, in one way or another. My book wouldn't be what it is without them. I won't name everyone, but hopefully by having this page it'll be fixed in life, for posterity, that you played a role, for which I'll be forever thankful.

All my family with their patience and advice.
So many of my friends who read various drafts and believed in me enough to be brutally honest.
The children who read the early drafts of both the book and the blurb, and who made the book real.
The friends who knew people, who knew people, who could help me with whole task of self-publishing, a task that goes way beyond uploading a document.
The acquaintances, who have since become friends, who have helped me get my book out into the world.

And Tom Mankin, my illustrator. He brought my book to life with his beautiful, clever, playful artwork; his ability to attune to the characters and the nuances of my book was simply amazing.

Thank you.